a PORTHKENNACK
CONTEMPORARY

FOXGLOVE COPSE

ALEX BEECROFT

RIPTIDE
PUBLISHING

Riptide Publishing
PO Box 1537
Burnsville, NC 28714
www.riptidepublishing.com

Foxglove Copse
Copyright © 2017 by Alex Beecroft

Cover art: G. D. Leigh, blackjazzdesign.com
Editors: Sarah Lyons, Carole-ann Galloway
Layout: L.C. Chase, lcchase.com/design.htm

ISBN: 978-1-62649-547-0

First edition
September, 2017

Also available in ebook:
ISBN: 978-1-62649-546-3

a PORTHKENNACK
CONTEMPORARY

FOXGLOVE COPSE

ALEX BEECROFT

RIPTIDE
PUBLISHING

*To all the anxious people reading this, my admiration,
because you know all the ways in which it could go wrong,
and you do it anyway. That's bravery in its essence.*

TABLE OF
CONTENTS

CHAPTER ONE

Sourton Cross service station had a picnic site with toilets, a shower, and an outside potable water tap. Luxury. Sam Atkins stopped there under a sky as downcast as his future. He parked the van as close to the toilet block as possible and filled his water tank with a hose he was almost too numb to feel, his fingers livid white with cold where they poked out of his red-and-black fingerless gloves.

That done, he took a damp and comfortless towel into the chill ceramic loos in search of warm water and free soap. Not unexpectedly, it smelled of mould and piss and mud inside. The floor was wet with boot prints, and the tray of the shower half-silted with sand and leaves. Some large dog, perhaps, had been sluiced down there before bounding back into its owner's warm, carpeted four-by-four.

But Sam had been on the road for nearly half a year and had come prepared. He let the water run for a while, to take the worst of the dirt down the plughole, then he took flip-flops and a large plastic bag from his pocket. Stripping, he put his clothes on the bag, stepped from his boots into the flip-flops, and got into the shower moments before the unforgiving December air took all the breath from his body.

Hot water! An unceasing flood of it, kneading his scalp and soothing his shoulders. This time last year he'd had a wet room, in a house, a room finished in marble, with a power shower of gleaming copper, the size of a hubcap. If he closed his eyes, here in this cold winter car park, the sense of decadence was the same. But with the memory came the choking sensation that he had also felt in that room, while trying to wash off panic, sleeplessness, and stress.

He opened his eyes to find a mottled brown terrier nosing at his coat, a bespectacled man at the nearest urinal watching him out of the corner of his eye.

"All right?" he challenged.

The man looked away, but Sam's brief moment of indulgence was undone regardless. He kept the water running for the warmth of the steam as he stepped out, rubbed the clammy towel over himself, and struggled to pull back on the clothes he'd been wearing since the launderette in Hackney, over a fortnight ago.

He had no idea what kind of perversions or judgements were going through the bespectacled man's head, but he breathed easier when the guy left, taking his mongrel dog with him. Now he could at least dry his hair and his towel under a hand drier in peace.

It felt good to be clean. These days, even that was an achievement.

Outside, the light had faded further, and it had begun to rain. He put up his hood and sprinted for the van, getting through the door and into the driver's seat before he lost all traces of warmth. Starting her up, he moved from just outside the toilet block to just outside McDonald's, checking his phone while he tried the three closest spaces one after another.

A glance in the driving mirror said he still looked shaggy, suspicious, so he plugged his electric shaver into the cigarette lighter. A number-one comb took the beard down to designer stubble, and a number sixteen cropped his fair hair until it was only beginning to show a curl.

There. Now, with the Barbour waterproof coat and hat left over from better days, the Aran sweater and the briefcase containing his laptop, he passed for a gentleman farmer. Someone who wouldn't be side-eyed in the toilets by the respectability police.

Inside McDonald's, everything glowed warm and bright—a different culture, one to which he no longer belonged. Jingly Christmas music, the smell of fat, and the rumble of people talking. Red and yellow plastic toys in a glass display cabinet. Green plastic on the chairs, sticky with spilled sauce—the details assaulted him. The inside of the windows had steamed up; the whole place was crammed with bodies breathing the same air, and Sam's heart got stuck somewhere in his viscera, tangling them up until he thought he was going to puke.

"How can I help you?" said the plump Indian girl at the till for the second time, breaking him out of his spiral. Goddamn it, he had to fake normality better than this.

He smiled. "Sorry. Miles away. Um, just a white coffee please."

Pressing his card to the contactless reader, he tried to effect the nonchalance of a man who had all the money in the world and no cares. No one liked to give you things if they thought you were actually in need. "And, uh, can I have the wi-fi password?"

He downloaded his emails sitting in the free warmth, sipping at the coffee for as long as he could make it last, then he returned to his van, where he made sandwiches, wrapped himself up in his quilt, and piggybacking on the wi-fi signal that spilled over to the car park, made the Skype call that he'd been putting off since November the first.

His mother picked up. He could see her in a brightly lit box in the corner of his screen, artfully made up, her beautiful silver hair feathered around cheekbones that still turned heads. "Sam! Oh my God, where are you now?" She literally clutched her pearls, which he had the resilience to find amusing.

"Hi, Mum." A tiny point of pain flowered under his right shoulder blade, as though someone had just pierced the skin there with the point of a pickaxe, and was driving in with excruciating slowness. "How are you doing?"

"Sam," she said, warningly. "Don't take that tone."

He smoothed his fingers through his newly shaven beard, reminding himself that he had achieved something today. He was not—yet—a complete failure. "What tone?"

"The tone where you keep pretending that nothing's wrong. When are you coming home? When are you going to come to your senses and find a new job? You can't drive around parking in lay-bys for the rest of your life."

"Short answers?" Long answers would have taken a novel, one for which he didn't have the words or aptitude. "I'm not. I'm not. And yes, I can."

"Yes, of course you can." Her grey eyes were as sharp as the points of stilettos. "How are you going to keep feeding yourself? Buying petrol—"

"Diesel," he coughed, as though it had been driven out of him by the skewer that was still pushing through his back. Axminster carpet was visible over his mother's tailored shoulder, and the long scarlet edge of *Three Sunflowers and a Bottle of Water* by David Hockney, which she had bought from him when he had been selling off the contents of his house.

"Same thing," she snapped. "My point is that by now the paltry amount you kept for yourself after your episode must be running out. I understand that you had a shock, and you've needed time to get over it, but really, I am beginning to be seriously concerned about your mental welfare, Sam. You can't carry on the way you're going. You must come home."

"Is that Sam?" He recognized his sister's voice, sounding tinny at a distance. Tabitha eclipsed the red line of the painting as she strode into the webcam's view and waved: tall and even fairer than him, impeccably suited, with the gleam of permanent triumph in her green eye. "Have you starved to death yet, darling? Do you need me to lend you a couple of thousand?"

"Sam!" His mother must have caught the look on his face. "Don't hang up. Tabby, go and sit somewhere else."

For a marvel, Tabitha did, though her long legs in their Christian Louboutin shoes poked into the upper corner of the frame. She had been the underachiever when Sam had been earning fifty thousand pounds a year plus an extra fifty thou' in bonuses, and now she was the family's darling. She did so enjoy reminding him of it.

"I know you've been having some problems, emotionally," his mother continued, as though she were gingerly picking up a disgusting rag. "We can fix that. Come home. Come home for Christmas, at the very least, and we can start finding the right medication for your anxiety problems. Daddy can find you an easier job. A nice little flat. You can start again, here where we can help you."

By now the skewer through his back had expanded to the diameter of a golf ball, all the muscles around it locking down in panic. He could barely gasp a shallow breath around the unyielding pressure of it, this imaginary pain that felt like a spear through the lung. "I've got to go."

"Don't do this to me, Sam. How can you be so selfish?"

He shut the computer down and curled up. Breathing, breathing in the quiet, wood-lined room that was the back of his converted van, with the blind down over the rear window so he wouldn't be seen.

It was true that he had three hundred and seventy-five pounds eighty-four pence to his name, and he didn't know what he would do when it ran out. But if he found somewhere more permanent to stop, he could certainly eke it out until after Christmas. He could not bear to put himself in their clutches for the season of goodwill.

A half an hour later, he came back to himself to find he was watching the rain snake in silver serpents down the windscreen. As his brain rebooted, he discovered he was tired but ready to move on. Slipping into the driver's seat, he started her up, easing back out into the A30 traffic with no clear destination in mind. Maybe Bodmin. Perhaps he could stop somewhere on the moor and live in a neolithic shepherd's hut, like Sherlock Holmes.

But Bodmin was featureless and grey in the rain, with a bleakness he didn't need on top of his own. On a whim, he turned up the B3274 and headed towards Porthkennack instead.

As if by omen, the rain slackened as he came within sight of the sea, and the sunset drew brief bands of gold across the horizon. The road crested a small hill, from which he could see down into a galaxy of homely windows, and afar off the silent pulse of a lighthouse.

To his left, a gap in the hedgerow beckoned. He slowed, the only vehicle on the road, and turned his lights to it. Yes. There was a faint track. Beyond it, a swaying shadow against the stars, was a woodland, where the glint of a brook vanished into glossy rhododendron and the low, broad leaves of foxgloves open like imploring hands in the gloom.

Running water and camouflage—he might stay there for some time without being seen. Making an instant decision, he rolled gently up the bank and carefully, carefully into the wood.

Three trees in, a fallen stump leaned across the track. At one point the wheel ruts had continued out into the distant fields, but it seemed that when the tree fell, the path had been abandoned to grow ferns and briars. That suited him; no one would be coming in or out. He would not be blocking anyone's access if he stayed here awhile.

Turning the engine off, he grabbed his torch from the glove box and stepped out into a shocking silence. No cars moved on the unlit road and the sky was end to end with stars, bleak and magnificent as the glitter of an iceberg. For a moment, it felt as though time itself had stopped, that he was the only human left in the universe. A chill crawled up his back.

But then the wind swept from the sea and sighed through the treetops around him. The moment passed as he folded out the mast for the wind-turbine and connected it to its battery.

Fallen branches littered the ground. He picked up some sprays of rhododendron and leaned them against the van's green side, camouflaging it. Walking back to the road, he looked in and could not see her. Good. The concealment might not survive the coming of the dawn, but he should at least be able to sleep in peace.

He collected branches for the wood burner and stacked them in the passenger side footwell to dry out, laid his laptop on the fold-out table, and considered browsing the job sites for temporary work nearby. Just the thought of it narrowed his chest until he couldn't squeeze in a breath. Clocking in at a regular time, talking to people, pay cheques, responsibility . . .

Turning his back on everything, he decided to take a walk and then go to bed early. Maybe, when he'd had a good night's sleep, he could face his future.

Barely five minutes' walk down the overgrown, abandoned path, the wood gave way to rough grazing land on a one-in-seven slope. Once he had come out of the trees, he could see down, in shades of dun and grey, past humps of rocks, to the solid black presence of a distant farm house, with lights burning behind its windows. The flecks of white scattered across the hillside must be sheep.

It took him a while of watching the fluffy white dots move, sweeping in one scatter from a nearby epicentre, before it occurred to him that this was not how sheep normally behaved. The baas that gusted to his ears on the wind were high-pitched and full of panic. Something had spooked them—something over by that cluster of rocks.

Curiosity drove him down the rough hummocks of the tussocky slope, heather and grass slippery under his wellies, his wind-up torch dimming as its charge ran out. The circle of light turned to umber and vanished altogether. He didn't wind it again, because the moon and stars were shining brightly. He could see enough, and he didn't want to be seen.

As he approached the rocks, he saw with a lurch of foreboding that they were not just tumbled there by the landscape. Five of them stood up on their narrow ends like the fingers of a buried hand, and in the centre of the "palm" something dark and small lay.

He thought it was another stone at first—an altar stone, where tens of thousands of years ago the neolithic people here had placated their gods. But then the gusting wind brought the smell.

Before, the night had been all newly washed rock and grass, distant seaweed. Now, his already unsettled stomach writhed inside him like a hatching alien, because this was a warmer scent. Blood. Blood and shit and acrid fear—the smell of death.

Why he ran forward, he didn't know. Maybe to help. But the animal in the stone hand was past help. One of the sheep, its white coat so sodden with blood that even under the moon it did not gleam. It lay on its back, the rib cage cut open with ugly, tearing wounds, the bones severed at the back so that it could be opened like a flower to show that all of the organs had been removed.

CHAPTER TWO

Above the sheep's head, a circle of stones and twigs marked out a pentagram, with symbols at its points. Academic curiosity pricked Sam out of his automatic recoil, made him put his boot back down with a squelch in what he now realized must be a swamp of blood. Instead of running away, he leant down over the mark to try to puzzle it out.

Six months on the road. He'd had plenty of time to delve deep into the arcana of the internet and study the things that interested him. One of which was the occult. If someone had copied this from a design on the web, they had not made a very good job of it. He couldn't work out what it was trying to achieve. None of these sigils made any sense.

Sam was winding up his torch again when he heard a *click* behind him—the sound of a shotgun barrel being snapped into place. He stood up and raised both hands even before one voice said, "What the—" and the other growled, "All right, then. You turn around."

Keeping his hands by his ears, he did as they suggested. There were two of them. The older woman must be the farmer—straight silver hair under a flat cap, her face baked by an outdoors life, straight brows, straight mouth, and an implacable steeliness in the dark eyes. She held the shotgun with an ease that spoke of years of practice. Probably potting rabbits and winging poachers from the day she was born.

The second was a younger man in a town dweller's impractical coat and trainers. In one hand, he held a lantern, the yellow light of which gilded the curls of his black hair and brought a sheen of amber to his kindly grey eyes,—worried, uncertain, and startling. His other hand rested gently on the head of a nervous black-and-white sheepdog.

"Drop what you're carrying," said the woman, voice harsh with rage and hurt.

Sam didn't think the young man would let him be shot. There was something very reassuring about him, standing there with his light like a romantic allegory. "It's—"

"Drop it!"

Sam dropped the torch and backed away as youth and dog came forward to pick it up.

"It's just a torch," he explained, seeing the young man puzzle over the fold-out wheel on the side. "You wind it up, so it doesn't need batteries."

The farmer barked out a bitter laugh; clearly she was not there to discuss the latest gadgetry. "What the hell d'you think you're doing with my sheep?"

A fine tremor vibrated up Sam's backbone, down his legs to his knees, and in every particle of his lungs, but oddly enough the clench of his anxiety had eased. Plain threat was not sneaky enough to terrify him. "I'm not doing anything," he said. "I went out for a walk. I saw the sheep tearing away from this place, so I came to see what had frightened them. And I found . . ." He gestured at the corpse. "I was examining it when you arrived."

"Right," the farmer mocked. "This here's none of your doing? Expect me to believe that do you? Corpse is still steaming, and you're a stranger. Now, I can call the police, or you can pay me what she was worth and then get the hell off my land. Which is it going to be?"

"It is a torch, though, Auntie Jennifer. See?"

The young man with the light had been winding all this time. Now he flicked Sam's torch on, illuminating his own green University of Truro sweatshirt and the hand-knitted rainbow scarf wound copiously above it. Out-of-touch Christian hippy? Or gay? Sam flicked him a thankful glance regardless, but hoped for option two.

"And look," he turned the beam on Sam, sweeping it over his hands and the cuffs of his white Aran sweater that poked out beneath his coat. "There's no blood on him."

Sam had only just begun to wake to the fact that he was in trouble. He didn't know how much a sheep cost, but was sure he couldn't afford to pay for it. And the police? If he got involved with the police, his family would instantly sweep in, deprive him of his liberty, and set about retraining him to their own lifestyle once more. And that would kill him. It would outright kill him. He shuddered.

"Thank you," he offered the young man a somewhat pleading smile. "Also, notice that the organs are gone, and I don't have them. Whoever did this must have taken them away with him."

"Ruan, you get behind me with the dog." Jennifer jerked her chin to her nephew, then motioned with the shotgun, indicating that Sam should start walking down towards the farmhouse. Sam took a step to indicate willingness, wondering if he should break for it—if the woman would miss her shot in the dark. If he would have time to start the van and back it out of that narrow gap before the locals could catch up with him.

No. She'd just shoot the wheels, and then he'd have tyres to pay for too.

"If you look at the rib cage," he said, stopping, "you can see where it's been cut away from the spine. I think whoever did it must have had a chainsaw. I don't have a chainsaw."

"Then what the hell *were* you doing? You were leaning right over the thing when we got here. What d'you do that for, then, Sherlock, if you weren't doing no wrong?"

"These symbols." Sam cast a look of appeal Ruan's way, took off his wide-brimmed rain hat to let the wind ruffle his newly fluffy, newly cut hair, in case that would sway the young man further in his favour. "I have an interest in the history of the occult, and I wanted to see if I could understand the working that was being performed here. I mean, it's a sacrifice, obviously, but you'd expect it to say who to, and what it was meant to achieve."

Auntie Jennifer gave another bark of laughter, though even she was now scanning the ground around them as if she hoped to find the missing viscera neatly piled beside one of the standing stones. "Right. So what you're saying is that two people who understand this kind of witchcraft turned up here tonight, at the very same time, and you're the good one."

"What do you mean 'at the same time'?" Sam asked, his bravery taking a sudden drop, hollowing out his stomach with it.

"Them sheep," Jennifer nodded at them. The distant flock had dispersed and were now slowly wandering and grazing as Sam would have expected of them. "It weren't more than a moment after I saw 'em bolt that I came up and found you. If you didn't do it yourself, he must still be round here, with his chainsaw and his bag of guts. You must've seen him go."

"Or he saw me coming," Sam whispered. "Oh my God!" He had so little left in the world, only Diane the green van, and his laptop. His state-of-the-art MacBook Pro. "I had my torch on. Maybe I startled him? If he heard me coming across the field, he would have looked around and seen you two with your lantern."

If he couldn't afford to replace a sheep, or a tyre, he most certainly could not afford a new laptop, and the laptop was his only link home, his only link to the rest of the world. He didn't count the phone— He couldn't search for jobs or code or do his banking or . . . or live without his laptop. "Oh my God, I left the van unlocked. I've got to go and make sure it's all right. I've got to. Please."

CHAPTER THREE

"So you're admitting that you're squatting on my land without permission?" Jennifer narrowed her eyes at Sam, like a woman who'd had just about enough for one evening.

Sam knew how that felt. Already there was something in his chest, tightening around his windpipe and his heart. Some bastard of a thing that never killed him but did everything it could to make his life miserable. *"Stress, darling,"* his mother had said dismissively when he'd mentioned it to her. *"Everyone has that."* But how could anyone ever know that they were having a heart attack, in that case, if the feeling of being strangled in the chest was so very common?

"I only meant to stop for the night," he said, wheezing around the constriction in his throat. "Please. I'm trying to live off-grid, sustainably, you know? I could see the copse wasn't being used, so I thought no one would mind if I stayed until the morning. And then I came out for a walk and found this. Please."

Ruan raised his lantern and came a step closer. His slenderness had misguided Sam into thinking him small, but as he closed the distance between them, Sam had to raise his head to meet his eyes. They were grey eyes, like water under starlight, in a face whose long nose and long chin put him in mind of a curious puppy, nosing him out to see if he would play.

Maybe the young man could see that he was desperate and frightened and no threat, because his mouth quirked up a little at the edges, and that was all it took to give him the air of the friend that Sam had not known he needed. "Why don't we go and look, Auntie Jennifer? Maybe the guts and the chainsaw'll be there and then we'll know."

The van door stood ajar when they reached the copse. Sam's torch caught the edge of it, and the spot of light fluttered all over the clearing as his hand began to shake. He had to stop and bend over, panting to get air into his lungs. The whole of his back had turned to stone, and his ribs were metal bars that ached as if they'd been dunked in liquid nitrogen. When Ruan put a hand under his elbow, he all but jumped three feet.

"Are you on something?" Ruan asked, his voice lowered, presumably so that Jennifer wouldn't hear. She had already reached the door and pulled it fully open, letting the light from inside spill out into the night, and peered in before she stepped inside.

"No," Sam managed, struggling not to zone out or to scream. "I get . . . anxiety. It's like . . . It hurts. I just need . . . everything to stop."

Ruan tightened his grip, reassuringly, letting that lopsided smile gleam out again. "Not your night, eh? If you're a sheep-mutilating cultist, you want to move into a different line of work, certain sure."

"I'm not—" By sheer force of willpower, Sam propelled himself another step forward, into the long rectangle of gold light spilling into the clearing from the lamp on his fold-down table. His empty fold-down table.

Where the laptop had been, there was now a pair of reddish-brown smudges, such as might have been made by fingers in bloody gloves. The MiFi dongle—which allowed him to connect to the internet out here—had been knocked free and had fallen onto his seat, drawing his eye down, beneath the table. There, sagging with a horrible suggestion of liquidity, an unfamiliar black plastic bag squelched when Jennifer yanked it free.

"Oh my God!" Sam didn't want to see what was inside—had to see what was inside. Had to know. Didn't want to know. "What—"

Jennifer unknotted the loose knot in which the bag was tied and eased its mouth open. Even in the cold winter air, the gust of warm meat scent was sickening. Ruan's lantern light picked out swells of smooth ruby organs like gory giant kidney beans, and long grey ropes of intestine, and folded, bleeding things that were probably lungs, and then Sam was wrenching his arm out of Ruan's grip and running, running.

No! the sane watcher in his head told him. *Don't do that. They'll think you're guilty. They'll think you've got something to hide.*

But that in itself just made him want to run more, to get away. He had to get away!

The ground was soggy, waterlogged, treacherous. Old fallen branches were everywhere, and where they weren't, the hummocks and dried stalks of foxgloves deceived his footing, tugged at the lacing of his boots.

A metallic *click* behind him, and a sheet of ice water seemed to break over his head and freeze his belly. His whole spine shuddered. That was Jennifer taking the safety catch off her shotgun.

Don't run! Don't run! whined the voice of his superego. *Damn you. Are you mad?* And now even his most level-headed part was off, panicking about exactly how insane he was and how the hell it was going to rein him back before he was shot, or just went permanently insane and ended up in an institution somewhere.

"I can't," he choked out, his ankle turning under him on the uncertain ground. "I can't—"

Couldn't what? Couldn't think, for a start. Oh God, now he was panicking about how badly he was panicking, in a recursive, sickening spiral he couldn't stop or slow down. Putting out both hands in front of him, he seized the bole of a tree and pressed his face into it.

Cold.

Cold.

Damp.

Solid.

Real.

He closed his eyes and clung on as he might have clung to a life raft in the middle of a stormy sea. Anchored, he tried to get a grip on his breathing. Failed. Tried again.

An odd patch of warmth on his lower back helped, spreading comfort like a hot water bottle pressed against an aching nerve. This time when he grabbed for his breathing, he caught it. Although it was like trying to wrestle himself into the driver's seat of a car being driven by a heart-attack victim, he was eventually able to get back the wheel from his lizard brain, put his foot down on the brakes, and with long, wrenching, continuous effort, slow everything down until he could almost pass for normal.

"Maybe you *should be* on something." Ruan's voice startled him, close to his ear and concerned. When he thought he could open his eyes without losing it, he did so, and found Ruan hunkered down next to him, one hand on his shoulder, the other slid under his coat and resting in the hollow of his spine, reassuring, warm and still. "Meds of some kind."

"I'm— It's normally not this bad," Sam whispered, shivery and aching for a cup of tea and blankets. Not prepared to think about his laptop yet, but very aware that he *wasn't* thinking about it. "I went in for the off-grid life because it's . . ." the chuckle threatened to become a full-blown hysterical cackling fit, but he put his foot down on that too, held on, "low stress. But I. I write code to keep me calm—shareware, you know? Websites and apps I can improve and give away. It's soothing. I need my laptop for that. I don't—"

"Did you kill Auntie Jennifer's sheep?" Ruan withdrew his warming hand to tuck back a windblown strand of hair behind his ear. His curly dark hair was too long for fashion, too short for a statement. It looked soft, and so did his expression. Suspicion would have sent Sam into another spiral, but this gaze of friendly concern made it feel safe to reply.

"I really didn't. I don't know who did, but whoever it was must have come back this way. They took my laptop, and they left the—" oozy innards "—stuff to make it seem like it was me. But it wasn't."

"I'm going to have a rummage for that chainsaw," Jennifer announced at high volume, and then paused as though this had been less of a statement, more of a request for permission.

"Okay." Sam rubbed his open hands over his face and nodded, gathering the strength to get to his feet. He staggered back closer to the van as Jennifer stepped inside, was scarcely aware that Ruan's hand was under his arm again, holding him up. They watched together as Jennifer opened all the cupboards, Sam picturing the contents as each was opened—the bedding folded under the floor, the dwindling stack of groceries beneath the sink, the tiny tiled shower room and toilet behind the driver's seat, the fold-out shelf of the bed.

Strangely, he could see Ruan beside him getting more and more upset. The young man's face paled, even his lips paled, and in the deep cold of the night, the smoke of his breath wreathed those starry eyes in mist.

"What?" Sam asked, as Ruan's mouth set downwards.

"Do you live here all the time?"

"Yes." Sam wondered what he'd done now. "Well, for the last six months."

"All alone?" Bemusement and horror mixed in Ruan's tone. "With no family, no people?"

Sam felt now like a saucepan left on the heat—he had boiled until he was empty and the residue of his emotions had stuck and burned. There was nothing left inside strong enough to counter the bitterness that welled up at the way Ruan said *family*. "They were the problem. Family! They fuck you up. You're better off without them."

It was extraordinary how much it hurt when Ruan let go of him and stepped away, looking like a worshipper whose sacred places had been trampled. He was probably one of those extroverts who thought the world revolved around relationships, who was never more happy than when he was surrounded by four or five generations of squabbling relatives.

"The English are weird." Ruan dismissed the subject in a voice that put an unwelcome distance between them, and addressed his next remark to Jennifer. "You find anything?"

She emerged from the van with the bag of guts in one hand and Sam's keys in the other. "I see no chainsaw, nor nothing else that could have made those cuts," she conceded, locking the door behind her. The straight lines of fury around her mouth echoed straight lines of puzzlement on her brow. "And it's true he'd have had to have sommat of the sort. Nor I don't see him keeping the offal and throwing away a good saw. Be more likely the other way around."

"What am I going to do?" Sam asked. Trying and failing to scrape together some dignity, he held out his hand for his van keys. "That laptop was my lifeline. I can't afford another one."

He squeezed his eyes closed against the sudden awareness of the hard square of his phone in his pocket. His mother's voice nagged in his head, telling him to phone home. To let them come and rescue him.

Dew settled lightly on his bare palm. He snapped his eyes back open as a jangle of untuned metal heralded Jennifer putting Sam's keys in her pocket. "What? My keys!"

"You come along down to the house with us." Jennifer's voice had lost a little ice but none of its implacability. "Looks like this is a police matter after all. You can wait for them there as well as here. I don't want you skipping out on us."

"Where would I possibly go?" Sam said wearily, surrendering to a life in which he had no say over anything. He followed them back out onto the star grey meadow, back to the standing stones, where Jennifer lowered the guts in their plastic bag back into their original owner.

"You sure it's not witchcraft?" Ruan asked Sam, watching this with his hand back between the sheepdog's ears. She had been whimpering at the smell ever since the bag came out of Sam's van. In the frosty light of the milky way, the pentagram over the dead sheep's head was surrounded by shadows so dark it might have been levitating above the ground.

Sam sighed. "Not really," he conceded. "A commonly held belief among Wiccans and witches of other traditions is that whatever energy you put out returns to you threefold. So ill-wishing someone would lead to you being harmed worse yourself. That tends to rule out trying to hurt people. But there are folk out there who don't believe in the rule of three. And there are people who will experiment with magic without joining a religion or a tradition, who therefore haven't been warned of potential consequences to themselves. It's a very diverse community. This sigil is nothing I recognize, but it could be a threat. Or a warning. Or a hex. I've got to assume that anything that involves killing your livestock without permission probably doesn't mean you well."

"You think it's a curse? On Auntie Jennifer?" Ruan's shiver was pronounced enough that Sam could watch its progress in the flex of his shoulders, the nervous twitch of his fingers. Belatedly he recognized that while he was intrigued by what he regarded as a fascinating intellectual puzzle, Ruan was genuinely afraid.

"Don't talk cack, you," Jennifer growled and pushed them both out of the stone circle and down towards the electric light of the house. "It's some sicko thief, nothing more."

CHAPTER
FOUR

"I don't need a babysitter!" Tegan crossed her arms and canted one skinny hip like an annoyed fishwife down by the docks.

Ruan gave a last wave and closed the door behind Aunt Meg and Uncle Phil, his mam's eldest sister and her husband, off for their weekly evening at the Sea Bell's folk music session. Normally his mam would come and sit with fourteen-year-old Tegan, but she had taken Jimmy to his gender clinic appointment in London and wouldn't be back till late.

"It's not much of a job," she'd said, handing it over to him that morning, while he had still been musing over the police interview, the horrible sacrilege of what had happened to Jennifer's sheep, and the stranger who was right down in the middle of it, claiming not to be involved at all.

"The little ones'll be in bed already and shouldn't stir. Tegan sits in her room on the internet with her friends. You sit downstairs and watch TV. About ten-ish you make some supper—hot chocolate, maybe, and toast, she likes. Meg comes home around midnight, 'less she's in a lock-in, and then you might need to sleep on the couch a bit. Always think it's a nice break, me."

"I'm not really here to babysit," Ruan reassured Tegan now, remembering how old and responsible he'd felt at fourteen, trying to soften the blow of his presence—the implication that Tegan's parents still considered her a child. "I'm hiding out."

Tegan uncrossed her arms and raised herself up onto the balls of her feet as if she were going to make a sprint for it, but there was an intrigued look in her slate-blue eyes. "From the police?"

"How do you know I'd been talking to the police?" Ruan shut the inner door of the small porch. The house was old, built in the eighteenth century onto the right side of the sixteenth-century fisherman's cottage that was Grandma Gwynn's. Gramma's had been recently modernized, when the family had come together to insulate the walls and roof, but Tegan's place was as it came, still: raw-boned and draughty. They didn't linger in the unheated, tiled hall, and Ruan was pleased when Tegan followed him into the sitting room, instead of going straight upstairs.

She plumped herself down on the sagging seventies sofa next to the hearth, and shivered pointedly. Taking the hint, he knelt by her and began to build up a pyramid of tinder and small sticks over a firelighter in the grate.

"Emily at school was up at Karen's house for a sleepover last night. Karen's dad said he'd been up at Auntie Jennifer's. Said there'd been 'an incident.' And you were up at Auntie Jennifer's last night too. So I . . ." She shrugged.

"And Karen's dad is in the police?" Ruan put the pieces together, while his hands moved automatically through the process of striking a match, touching the flame to the firelighter, and then balancing coal atop the stack of split wood. Put too much and you'd smother the fire. Too little and it would burn out before it got going.

"That's right." Tegan took the hair tie from her straggly, inky hair, scraped it back up and retied it so tight it must ache. "What kind of an incident was it? Are you in trouble?"

"I like the way you think it's my fault!" He poked her in the artful rip over the knee of her black jeans. The new fire was leaping up the kindling and smoking off the coal, and already a faint ghost promise of heat wisped from it, more than the best the radiators could do. "I was just a witness. I had to make a statement, but I'm not in trouble."

"What kind of an incident, though?" she insisted, folding out her laptop and plugging it into the four-way extension lead that trailed from the single plug by the door. The tell-tale hint of blue in the fraction of the screen he could see suggested that anything he said would be taken down in evidence on Facebook and spread among her friends.

It was still a relief to talk about it. "You know Jennifer's Alana's ill? That's why I went up, because Mam said Jennifer might need some help while Alana was too sick to go out?"

"Flu, I heard," Tegan agreed. "Here, Ruan, d'you think they're together? Jennifer and Alana, I mean. My mam says they're like sisters, but Dad says not to talk about it in front of me, so I think . . ." She rolled her eyes at the older generation. "I think they're lesbians."

With the fire now contentedly crackling its way through its baby food and reaching out for more, Ruan added extra coal and fetched his bag from the hall. A scent of grapefruit came in with him. He didn't want to gossip about Jennifer and Alana, who had always discouraged such speculation, but a restlessness and itchiness about his spirit said he had to let the other stuff out to someone. "Well, I don't know. That's their business, isn't it? Whatever they are—friends or lovers or something in between, they're nice people and important to each other. That's all we need to know."

"Guh." Tegan rolled her eyes at him. "When did you get so boring?"

"I thought I was telling you about the incident, not discussing people's private lives," Ruan huffed, getting out his tattoo gun and plugging it into the extension. As he'd hoped, the machine made her crane forward with interest, gave him a pause where he could change the subject. "Anyway, like I was saying, I went out with Jennifer to check her sheep, and one of them had been killed."

Tegan actually slid the laptop off her lap and got her feet under her, kneeling up with her elbows propped on the sofa arm, so she could look more closely at his face. "Killed, like . . . by a dog?"

Ruan brought a grapefruit out of his bag, vividly aware of the water-filled weight of it and its smoothness, the spicy scent. He had drawn a butterfly on it freehand in water-soluble felt tip before coming, and he was picturing how he would shade it to make it look real, to work with and not against the light and shade of the curve on which it would be placed.

Much better to think of that than the curve of empty ribs, or the distended bag of guts, or the pentagram that no one but him seemed to be taking seriously. He set up the gun carefully—practice needles that he sterilized each time even though he was only going to use them on fruit, keeping back his hoard of disposable ones for use on people. This would probably be the last go-around for these—they blunted fast, and the line lost its integrity, became blurred and ugly.

"Nah," he said, swallowing. So glad, all of a sudden, that she was there. So glad he'd had Jennifer and the dogs to sit with last night, and Mam, Jimmy, and Lora to breakfast with. How the hell did Sam Atkins cope with anything, all on his own in that van that was practically a solitary cell on wheels? Well, he didn't, certain sure. But what kind of a family made that life seem like the better option?

"Someone had killed it as a sacrifice, right there in the five maids' circle, with a pentagram over its head." Ruan probably shouldn't be sharing this stuff with a fourteen-year-old, but she'd hear of it anyhow in a day or two. Talk ran faster round Porthkennack than the electric round the national grid.

"No!" Tegan breathed, looking excited rather than afraid. "Like in the witchcraft museum?"

Boscastle witchcraft museum, just over the bay, was a popular field trip for the schools. Ruan remembered when his class had gone, and how mercilessly he'd been mocked after for being creeped out by it.

"Yes," he said, "just like that. You reckon someone's trying to curse Auntie Jennifer? Maybe because they think she's gay?"

Tegan put out a hand and tugged gently on the end of Ruan's rainbow scarf, as if to say *I see why that worries you*. Then she smiled reassuringly, though the warmth of it didn't quite reach her eyes. He had the impression that she was troubled too, somewhere deeper than she would talk about. "You know the same thing happened to Daisy Martins's sister's friend, Laura, and she was like all over the boys. I mean, not the same thing, exactly. It was a crow, in her case, left on the doorstep, but she ain't gay, not a bit of it."

He tried putting down an antenna, the buzz and vibration up his arm beginning to feel comforting now as he adjusted to the machine, as art found a way to pass through his flesh and out of his fingers. This helped too—he felt less jittery if he could not allow his hands to shake. But this news was significant, wasn't it? He should consider this.

"Are you certain? They opened up the body and put a sign over its head?"

"Mm-hmm. She's not the first neither. They don't tell anyone, but that was the reason the Roscarrock twins went away to boarding school. They practically fell over something similar, just outside where they'd made a den in the garden. That was a cat though, I heard, and I think their mam were scared something bad would happen to them if they stayed."

"That was . . ." He had not jumped or screwed up the line. He was quite proud of himself. "But they left three years ago."

"Yeah." Tegan gave him a *well, duh* look. "So?"

He'd wanted to believe Sam, but he hadn't been fully able. Now he was taken aback by how much it mattered to him—what a relief it was to know for certain that the sheep killer couldn't have been Sam Atkins after all. He'd seen the tyre prints of the van standing up knife-edged in the mud, obviously fresh. He'd placed a hand on the bonnet and felt the tepid warmth of an engine that had only just begun to cool down. Whatever else you could say of the man, it was absolutely certain that he was newly arrived.

Which meant he couldn't have been responsible for an atrocity that happened three years ago. If there was a history of this stuff, then it was being done by someone else.

And if it was being done by someone else, then he didn't need to feel guilty about feeling sorry for Sam. The guy had come to Cornwall for refuge and immediately had his most valuable possession stolen. His "lifeline." It was obvious he needed one.

He was a nice-looking guy, too. Fair as a child and jumpy as one, but with the height and hard bones of a man. There'd been that about him, as he stretched up from stooping over the glyph, and the light from Ruan's lantern had picked out the long, robe-like coat and the wide brimmed hat, that put Ruan in mind of a wandering wizard. A hermit-in-the-wilderness, fantasy mentor vibe, though he was too young, too handsome to pull it off properly. "Hot techno-Merlin" was not Ruan's usual thing, but he had to admit he was intrigued.

"We thought for a while it might have been this emmet— eco-warrior type. He's camping out in Foxglove Copse, and he claims to know everything about magic and more about computers. But he's only just arrived, so he can't have been terrorising people for the last three years."

"Terrorising?" Tegan repeated thoughtfully, her gaze thrown down as she picked at the tear over her knee. "I . . ."

The syllable had a confessional air. Trying to be encouraging, he stopped his tattoo machine, but the silence that fell in the absence of its friendly buzzing felt stark, a mistake.

"I got to go to a funeral tomorrow," Tegan said, unexpectedly. "Linda Tyhiddy. I didn't like her much. No one really did. But she killed herself. It was you talking about terror made me think of it. I don't want to go, but I know I should." Her chin crumpled briefly and then firmed back up. "I mean, I know we should have been there for her before, when it mattered, but . . . Will you come?"

He got off his knees at once and swooped in to hug her. Just short, like. Reassuring. She was a good lass, and he was touched to be asked. "Of course I will, maid. Of course I will."

CHAPTER FIVE

Tegan's whole school had turned out for the funeral, and St. Ia's church bulged at the seams with teenagers. Coming in out of the frosty morning to a scarcely less cold interior, Ruan spotted Tegan in the second row of pews to the front. The boy on her left, who kept jogging her elbow as she tried to text, was Nasir Achmed, no doubt fidgeting in protest at being forced into church. The girl on her right was his older sister Maryam, incongruous in her hijab, who kept leaning across Tegan to whisper to her brother.

Tegan flashed Ruan a look full of compressed meaning, before turning back to her little screen. He gathered that she was glad he'd turned up, but she didn't want him to come over. She was in her own world, surrounded by her own people, and probably couldn't afford the loss of face she would incur if everyone knew she'd asked him for support.

Hard to believe it had been a whole ten years since he'd been that age and that raw under the eyes of his peers. Time did funny things. It felt like you were always the same age, and you just slid gently through the available roles. When he'd left for university, he'd been the kid who needed to be cared for. Now he was the protecting adult. Weird.

But not bad. Truth be told, he quite liked it. These days he could see himself settling down to one place. Finding a job. He'd ask at the tattoo shop in town, if he owner wasn't a Lusmoore, and the shop probably just a cover for something he didn't want to get involved in. But he could set up his own, perhaps. Maybe move in to one of the flats Auntie Meg had made out of Phil's grandad's house that had come down to them in his will.

Be nice to find someone to share it all with too. He'd had his share of one-night stands and raves and parties over the past three years, and the novelty had begun to wear off. Nice to have someone like his mam and dad did. Like maybe Jennifer and Alana did. Someone to look after him when he was sick and cheer on his successes when they came. Because it was all very well being the grown-up, but even grown-ups needed support every now and then.

The thought brought him to his feet against the back wall of the church as the pall-bearers came in, with their three-quarter-size coffin, all glossy and black. Pink flowers trembled on top of it, in a wreath that encircled a small white teddy bear with a pink bow tie.

If you didn't have people, you ended up like this. All of a sudden, though he didn't know the girl, he found himself on the point of tears. No fourteen-year-old should have come to this, with her whole life ahead of her. She had been barely more than a child. Had she had no one to talk to? No one to sit in the shadows behind her to give her moral support? No one to say, *It's okay. I know the world's scary, but it can be good. Try it, and I'll be here to catch you if you fall*? Why not?

As the congregation sat for the first reading, he could see that Nasir had gone very pale and still. Tegan and Maryam were sobbing, passing a lavender silk scarf between them as a handkerchief. The dead girl's parents in the front pew looked as though they had arrived from a different universe and were lost. Incomers to the area, they hadn't enough relatives in the town to fill up one pew. And now they had one less.

God. It was as much for his own sake as Tegan's that when the short sermon was over and the service moved outside, he took advantage of the milling around to step up to Tegan's side and brush her shoulder with his own. Nothing too affectionate—nothing that would get her called a baby when the class went back to school—but enough to remind her that he was there, and that only a phone call away was the whole Gwynn clan. All of them on her side.

She sniffed and rubbed her eyes on the cuff of her blue school shirt. Maryam had drifted aside, taking the scarf with her.

"Hey," Ruan said, sotto voce, aware that the interaction was drawing some glances and cutting it as short as he could. "Not long now."

"You better not talk to me here." Tegan shied from him, her stride stuttering, as though she wanted to push past and to stay close to him both and her body couldn't decide which. Her face was pinched around the red eyes. "I don't know who might be watching."

The coffin was being brought out of the church, baby's breath and blush roses trembling on its polished surface, and again Ruan could barely breathe. Pity and a generalized anger against the loss of an innocent life froze hard in him into a more cutting dread.

"Are you okay?" he persisted, reaching out to take Tegan's arm. "Is there something going—"

"I'm not talking to you right now." She snatched herself away and went running to Maryam's side, two rows back from the open mouth of the grave.

Unsettled, Ruan trailed the last stragglers to the graveyard. If there was a story here, a threat, he would get it out of Tegan later, when she was willing to talk. For now, he would let Linda have her day undisturbed.

He breathed in deep of the cold, ice-clear air and let the breath out, looking away from the mourners and the school friends, out past St. Ia's and to the sea behind it. Frost had polished the mirror of the day, and everything seemed to shine, from the grey old moss-covered crosses of the graveyard to the single bell in the small church's stubby steeple.

A blocky little stone building, hardly to be distinguished from a barn, St. Ia's had stood here since the sixth century, and her stones seemed to have risen out of the scrubby grass and silverweed all of their own accord.

That would be like Ia, if truth be told. An Irishwoman, she had apparently floated here on a miraculous leaf after having been left behind by her saintly companions for being too young for the job. Without setting foot here, she'd preached a sermon to the folk who had lived on the headland, and they had been so impressed, they had put up this church in gratitude.

Here in the summer, Linda could lie under a swath of flowers, pink spurge and purple restharrow, bright-yellow cowslip and white sandwort, and the sea would sigh on the rocks below, all silver and glister and bright aquamarine like it was today.

The thought ached his heart more than he liked. There were too many teenage girls in this story, all of them being held back or harassed in some way. God had intervened to make sure Ia got to do what she'd set her heart on, but Linda had not been so lucky. Was there more to her suicide than the pressures of everyday life? Why had she chosen to do something so drastic? Had someone put a snare in front of her feet too?

And what had Tegan done to make her so guilty and so skittish?

That was a terrible thought, and he hated himself for having it. He breathed on his chilled fingers, flexed his cold feet inside his shoes, and heard the rattling tap and thud of a shovel full of earth being tipped on top of a young life. His stomach twisted inside him like he was going to be sick, but the feeling was too heavy for that—it was the dread of death, the terror of what was unknown and unstoppable and inhuman.

It came up out of his memory like a jump-scare out of a horror movie—the thought of that pentagram. What if an influence had been brought through, out of that shadowy place on the other side of their rational daylight world. What if it was feeding, if it couldn't tackle a stringy old bird like Auntie Jennifer just yet and it was going after easier prey first?

What if I'm a credulous idiot?

Ruan shook himself, pulling his mind back from old superstitions and nonsense. He'd always had a vivid imagination—that was part of why he'd gone to art school, so he could learn how to get the fantasy out of his head and onto the page—but there was no call to let it rule his life.

He tucked his hands under his armpits to keep them warm—the frigid touch of the fingertips into his flanks made him shiver all over—and bowed his head for the priest's dismissal. Folk were already making their way down the hill towards the church hall, where a wake of tea and sandwiches had been promised.

He shouldn't be so fanciful, but he was not going to be complaisant either. If there was evil afoot, he would get to the bottom of it. One dead teen was one too many.

CHAPTER SIX

"One could hardly miss the fact that she was depressed."

Ruan had shaken the parents' hands as he came into the warmth of the shabby old church hall. He hadn't felt that they were touching him—there was a thin film of disconnect between his skin and theirs. Doubtlessly nothing was touching them right now. They were stuck in a silent bubble of grief and the rituals meant to soothe them were going on outside. *I'm so sorry,* he'd said. *If there's anything I can do to help...*

But there wasn't. It was far too late for that.

Now he found himself squashed into the corner of the hall where the spare tables had been stacked, a cup of tea in his right hand and a plate of cake in his left, and no hand left to eat it with. The ugly blue-painted radiators were putting out too much heat, so he'd taken off his coat and draped it over a table edge and perched himself there, out of the way, unremarkable and invisible.

The eddy of the crowd had brought two teachers close enough for him to hear their conversation. Mrs. Hathaway and Mr. McGreavy, maths and English, respectively. It was Mrs. Hathaway who had spoken, and who went on, in a suitably subdued voice, but with a disapproving tone. "It's been months since I could get the girl to lift her head in class, and the way she walked? Slouching like that? Practically a textbook case of being weighed down with something."

"I know . . ." Mr. McGreavy shook his bald head. "I blame myself to a certain degree. I could see—"

"Nonsense! Her parents should have dealt with it. They could have taken her to the doctor. I can't think why she didn't talk to them rather than let it get to this stage."

Ruan didn't know why he spoke up, but he couldn't stay silent. "Maybe she was gay," he said, startling them both. McGreavy's tea sloshed over the rim of its cup and pooled in his saucer as they turned simultaneously to peer at him as though he had materialized out of thin air.

"I'm sorry?"

"Maybe she was gay," Ruan repeated, remembering the terrible year before he came out to his parents, when he had tormented himself with thoughts of what it was going to be like as the school pariah, if even his family wouldn't stand by him. And he'd had good cause to know that his parents would be fine with it. "And she knew she couldn't talk to them about it because they'd turn on her. She should have been able to talk to her friends instead, or her teachers."

Mrs. Hathaway scoffed behind her scone. "She didn't have any friends. A most unattractive, unfriendly, painfully socially withdrawn young girl."

"That's not fair!" Maryam had drifted into the conversation's orbit and now looked astonished at herself, wringing her lilac scarf between her hands. She retreated a step as the teachers turned their attention on her, and Ruan gave her an encouraging smile on principle. "She was fine last year," she ventured, big-eyed, as if frightened to make her point but determined. "She was going to get a horse and enter dressage competitions. This wasn't *her* fault. Or her parents.'"

Mrs. Hathaway seemed to have been frozen by the surprise that a child had had the temerity to address her. She stirred out of it only reluctantly. "Well, I don't think on an occasion like this there is any cause to go around casting blame. These tragedies happen. We must simply gird ourselves up and go on. Excuse me."

With a huff, she detached herself from what had become a small knot of conversation and escaped towards the buffet. Mr. McGreavy gave an apologetic smile to Ruan and sloped off after her.

"Lot of good they are," Ruan remarked to Maryam once they'd gone. Maryam had the panda-eyed look of a girl who'd been crying in nonwaterproof mascara, and her scarf bore black smudges from wiping most of it off. That was natural enough on an occasion like this, but there was something else in the hollows of her cheeks—a hopelessness in the back of her warm brown eyes that he didn't like.

His heart had gone out to her already as a friend of Tegan's, but now it latched on for her own sake. "Are you all right?"

"She was bi," Maryam blurted, as though it had been tortured out of her. She smoothed the folds of her black hijab around her shoulders, around her ears, and then around her shoulders again—a long endless sweep of something to do with her hands.

Behind her back, Ruan saw Tegan put down an egg mayonnaise sandwich and begin to make her way towards him. He revisited his assumptions about which of the girls was protecting the other.

"I don't know how you know. She dursn't tell anyone."

"I didn't know," Ruan said, softly as he could and with a new pang for the dead girl. Another one of his people lost. "But I remember what it was like for me. I'm gay."

"I think that's bloody obvious, Uncle Ruan." Tegan had arrived. She slipped her hand under Maryam's elbow and squeezed. "I can't imagine there was a time before people knew about you."

"There was though," he said, thankful for her. Maryam had regained a tiny glint of humour in the side of her mouth, and he felt better too for Tegan's bolstering presence. "I remember, the year before I came out; it was so hard. I was scared of everything, and there were some boys . . ." It still made his heart race to think of them, and his stomach feel like it had dropped to his knees. "They suspected, and they made my life hell."

"What did you do?" Both the girls were looking at him like this could be it—this could be their salvation. If it could, well, he was at their service to go and menace whomever they pleased.

"I told my da, and he and Uncle Phil had a word with them. They kept it down after that. They knew I had people who knew where they lived."

"Oh." Maryam sighed. Her hands took up their circular sweep once more, and Tegan's shoulders dropped as her back slumped.

"Is someone giving you grief?" Ruan ventured. It felt impertinent, when the two girls were so clearly side by side against the world, to suggest that they might need anyone else, but the whole town had been too late for Linda. Never again. "Because I know I'm not scary, but you should see my auntie Jennifer with a shotgun. If someone's having a go at you, we can stop that, I'm sure."

Tegan took his empty cup from his hand and placed his plate down on a window ledge, scuffing the peeling blue paint. "We should go outside," she said, which he took as a yes. He shrugged his quilted coat on and followed her.

Outside, the wind had picked up and the clouds come over. It looked like winter now, properly, steel grey from one horizon to the next, the light gone down into an underwater griminess as tiny flecks of rain drove into their faces.

By an unspoken agreement, Ruan found himself walking with the two girls on the path that returned to the church. They had gone through the lich-gate and flinched away from the piled flowers around the fresh scar, where Mr. Hughes the sexton was patting down the new grave, before a nod from Tegan reopened the floor for discussion.

"It's no good," Maryam said, like a spectre in her long black coat and her black veil. "We don't know who's doing it."

"Someone's bullying you, but you don't know who it is?"

"That's right," Tegan agreed when Maryam didn't seem to want to go on. "We don't even know if it's one person or lots of 'em. Linda was the first, but—"

Ruan had a Seurat moment, when the dots came together of their own accord and he got the picture. "Someone *drove her* to this?"

Maryam's lilac hanky came out again. She pressed it to her eyes and made a strangled noise. "Telling her she was disgusting. Telling her she was lying and there was no such thing as bisexuals. Telling her she had to choose one side or another because she couldn't be both. Telling her she was going to hell. Mostly on the internet. And phones. Her parents said, 'Well, just don't go on social media, then,' but if you're not on it, you miss everything."

"You can't . . . block this person?" Ruan would be the first to admit he wasn't an internet guru. He only used his own laptop to keep up with family news on Facebook and browse Google Images for inspiration, but he knew enough to believe that sites were supposed to have safeguards against this sort of thing.

Tegan gave a *God, you're so out of touch* sigh. "You can block one account, and then they go and make another. And maybe there's lots of them behind it, and maybe it's just one sicko with lots of different names. We can't tell. We have to walk round school all day not knowing whether whoever it is we're talking to is involved or not. Not knowing who's listening. Not knowing who else he's getting at."

"And then we have to stand by her grave and wonder who's killing us. Who is going to go next." Maryam bared her teeth. "There's a fat girl in 4G, Sarah Richardson. She looks bad, but she won't say anything—"

"They say we'll be killed if we tell anyone," Tegan blurted out, her face very white and strained and her fists clenched, as though she'd decided that was it. If she was going to say anything, she was going to tell all and take the consequences. Ruan would have liked to laugh, to say, *That kind of thing doesn't happen here*, but the graveside of a dead girl was not the place for it.

"If it's all on the internet though," he did try, "that's probably just talk. I know it's horrible, but—"

"Don't!" Tegan snapped. "We weren't sure about telling you, but now we have, you take us seriously, all right? It's not all talk. We keep getting viruses, screamers. We don't know if he's got our bank details. I mean, we change passwords, but is that enough? I don't—"

"There was a . . ." He scarcely heard Maryam's whisper over Tegan's indignation, but something in the tone of it made him listen hard. "There was a threat written on my doorstep. It's someone we know certain sure. Someone who knows where we live."

"And you don't have any suspicions?" Abruptly, Ruan had a big problem with being the adult in this situation. What made them think that he knew what to do?

"Oh, we have *suspicions*, sure enough." Tegan glared. They both folded their arms. It was endearingly nonthreatening, like being menaced by kittens. "There's a dozen boys in the sixth form who think it's funny—might be any one of them. We want more than suspicions. We want proof. We want something we can take to the police and get the bastard punished."

The mention of the police triggered a memory of Sam Atkins trying to explain the importance of his laptop. Ruan had been intrigued and curious and wanting an excuse to go back and talk to Sam, who his own imagination had built up into some kind of techno-mage. You'd have to be, if you coded for fun, wouldn't you?

You'd have to at least have more of a clue than Ruan did, in the software line.

"Tell you what," he said, all his pieces coming together with a magnetic snap. "Why don't you go get your computer? Maybe there's a way to hunt down where the messages have come from. Find out the IP address—that's right, isn't it? And, like, make proper sure all the viruses've gone. I'm not much with computers myself, but I might know a man who is."

CHAPTER SEVEN

"All right, then. You understand that you're to report to the station on the fifteenth to redeem your bail?"

Sam nodded dutifully, barely keeping his eyes open. Since Jennifer, Ruan, and he had made statements, down in Jennifer's ancient kitchen, he had not been getting much sleep. There'd been some wrangling about where he would stay. If he was to be accused of sheep mutilation, then perhaps, Sgt. Quick had said, he should be in a cell until he could raise bail.

That had been the start of a long debate between Jennifer and Ruan and Sgt. Quick—whom Jennifer had referred to as Pete—that ended with the advice to let things lie.

"You want my opinion?" Pete had said, stretching out his steaming boots closer to the heat. "You'd make trespass stick, but anything else is circumstantial. I'll bind him over as a witness if you must take it to court, but I know you. You wouldn't be giving him tea if you really thought he was guilty."

There'd been an old grandfather clock by the door to the sitting room, and it ticked with a majestic regularity. Sam had closed his eyes and listened to the mechanism. He'd almost been able to parse out the separate knocks of the cogs and the rocker and the grasshopper escapement. Their intricate but predictable pattern had been soothing in the midst of the uncertainty of human interaction.

Oddly, he'd found the police presence calming too. Being powerless meant he didn't have to make decisions. He couldn't, therefore, make mistakes. He had surrendered to his fate with a sense of relief and let the locals carry him along.

"I want everyone to know that you don't come on my land and harm my stock and not pay for it." Jennifer was implacable, but she had still pushed a plate of biscuits towards Sam and let him bask in the free heat. "It's the principle of the thing, isn't it? I've been done wrong; I get to see someone in the dock."

"Even if it's not the right man, Auntie?" Ruan had taken off his big scarf, but the effect had been only to reveal wide shoulders, a little rawboned and coltish. There was something charmingly unfinished about him, as though he was poised right on the edge of becoming. Sam would have bet, if he were a betting man, that whatever it was he was becoming would not be as harsh as his auntie Jennifer.

Who had snorted at the accusation. "If I settle now, Pete here'll think it's all dealt with. That'll be the end of it as far as he's concerned. And maybe he'll look into this gentleman's lost computer, but he'll forget that someone's been up here working some unholy purpose with my sheep. So I am sorry, Mr. Atkins, but I'm going to charge you, if only so that'll give Pete the boot up the arse he needs to find out who really did it."

By the time Sam had his statement taken, his bail date set, and his keys restored, it had been two in the morning, and after the nervous exertion of the day, he was wrecked. He had slogged back up the cold field with water beginning to soak through the cracking soles of his boots, and crawled inside his van to shiver for another hour before he could sleep.

At nine in the morning, two different policemen woke him, hearty and unapologetic as they barged through his blearily opened rear door and began to search the van.

He'd watched them from his bed in boxers and vest, acutely ashamed of his late rising and his unconventional lifestyle and his inability even to offer them tea and biscuits because his cupboards were bare.

They'd stayed, picking over the copse for hidden chainsaws, throughout most of that day – long enough that he could not face even walking into town for supplies afterward. So dinner that evening was a cocoa-pop sandwich eaten morosely by a fire of damp, smoking wood. Exhausted, he had gone to bed early, slept fitfully, and was rudely catapulted into the day when they came back, this time at 6 a.m.

It was past noon now, and after having gone through his statement yet again, they were finally leaving, thank God. He had kept his temper the whole time, and all the different parts of his soul were yearning for the moment when they would be gone and quiet returned.

"Yes. I understand that I've got to turn up to redeem my bail," he said, accompanying them out to the turn off onto the road. "Ms. Gwynn says that I can stay here until then, so you know where to find me when the real culprit turns up. I won't be going anywhere."

"See that you don't," the constable said, and they got into a car whose strips of shiny yellow and blue paint reflected the last gleam of the sky in the east, before the clouds drew in.

When the police rolled away, Sam took a bruised deep breath that smelled of moss and mulch. A damp chill had closed in with the clouds, and the trees around him seemed to be soaking it up, shuddering as the wind touched the tips of their branches. It was even darker beneath them, and softer like the gloom beneath a blanket. Shivering, he boiled the kettle, ate a quick sandwich, made a hot water bottle, and went back to bed.

Again, it felt as though he'd barely touched his head to the pillow before someone was banging on the doors, making the toothbrush rattle in its glass in the tiny bathroom. Sam pulled his duvet over his cold ears and groaned. Exhaustion threatened to overwhelm him with nervous anger. Why the fuck couldn't everyone leave him alone to make up the sleep he so desperately needed? Why, when everything was so difficult, did someone inevitably make it worse? Didn't they know how hard he worked even at the best of times to hold himself together? Didn't they know how much he needed his sleep? How could they be so fucking thoughtless?

But three years of therapy had left him with some benefits. When his body curled up in fury with his hands clenched and his heart thundering in his ears and everything tasting of iron, he closed his eyes and said *no*.

No. This anger was not a true reflection of the situation he found himself in. The anger in itself was increasing his suffering, winding him tighter, adding to the overwrought pain at the back of his neck and across his shoulders.

Knock, knock. "Are you in there?"

He closed his eyes, took a deep breath, and put the anger down as carefully as he might have put down an irritated rattlesnake. He couldn't unknot the tension in his back, but could at least swing his bare legs out of the bunk and begin to draw on his cold trousers.

"Mr. Atkins? Are you in?"

Another breath and another release, letting it all go, and he scrabbled back enough control over his voice to shout, "Yes. Just a moment!"

Cold, damp boots next. Then he wrestled back into the jumper he had at least had the sense to wrap around his hot water bottle, combed his fingers through his hair, and opened the back door.

Already it was dark outside, and he didn't know what he felt to see Ruan Gwynn's long, angular face picked out against the windy dark in lamplit lines of gold, just as it had been the other night. It was a sweeter face than he'd remembered, or perhaps that was the expression—hopeful, shy, a little humorous. As though Ruan thought that having been involved in Sam's arrest meant they were all friends now.

Grimy and weary with sleeplessness and strain, Sam wasn't sure if he should growl at that assumption. He'd been stepped on enough for one day, hadn't he? But there were two children with Ruan. One at either side. A girl whose heart-shaped face had a smaller version of Ruan's Roman nose—the effect was strangely charming. Obviously a relative, she was scowling at him in a way that Sam recognized as nervousness. The second girl was prettier, plumper, with amber-touched brown eyes that fleeted up to his and then away again, leaving the impression that she had been weeping.

Abruptly he wished that he had straightened the bed and shut all the cupboard doors that the police had left open. He backed inside, sweeping the mugs from this morning into the sink, and knocking the door to the bathroom closed as he gestured them all to come in.

"Give me a moment."

He covered the bed with its slip coat and slid it on its cantilevered platform into the wall, bringing the table and bench chairs beneath the floor into play. "There. Now you can have a seat."

"Whoa." Ruan's relative laughed, bending down to peer at the cracks in the floor from which the whole assembly had folded. "That's so neat. Did you make that? And do you live here all the time? It's so cold."

"Tegan!" Ruan gave him a *Kids, huh? What can you do?* look, grey eyes pale gold in the light of his lamp. The twist of his wide mouth brought the blood unexpectedly to Sam's lips and belly in a flowering of want. He turned away, unsettled and delighted. That had been desire. He thought he'd lost that for good last year.

"I'm sorry to come knocking on your door so soon after . . . all that," Ruan started, sliding himself neatly onto one of the benches, putting the lamp on the tabletop. "I know I can't be your favourite person right now."

"Still not the worst," Sam said, truthfully enough. "I'm sorry about the cold. I would put the engine on and warm it up a little, but I can't afford to."

"No, *I'm* sorry," Ruan said again, actually looking it this time. From certain angles there was a real elegance to him. From others he was just ungainly. Sam rather enjoyed the puzzle of him—enjoyed watching.

"I don't want to intrude on your trouble," Ruan continued, "but you said you liked coding, and we have a computer problem we need help with. I could . . ." he bit his lip, "I could maybe pay you something for it."

The veiled girl turned round to slip a backpack from her shoulder. A computer bag with a padded compartment for the laptop and separate storage for wires. "I have an allowance. And birthday money coming up. I don't know how much you charge, but . . ."

"I don't know how much I charge either." Sam smiled at the old ASUS ThinkPad she brought out. How kind of Ruan to think of him. Was it an apology? It was a very delicate one, if so. "What's this about?"

"This is my niece Tegan and her friend Maryam," Ruan said, indicating them. "They, uh, they been having some trouble with internet harassment. Like bullying—"

"And viruses."

"And viruses, and they want to know who's doing it. If it's one person or lots of people. They think it's someone in the town, but can you find out for sure? Whoever's doing this, I mean? Can you stop 'em?"

That sounded like responsibility. Sam wasn't ready for it. Dread closed his throat and chilled the faint breath of warmth that had leapt up in him. "I . . . I can certainly reformat any laptops you think are affected and install better anti-malware, though I'll need you to bring them to me. As to tracking him down, that's a longer process. If he's at all good at disguising his server, it won't be easy. I'd have to know all the forums and chat rooms and websites where the activity takes place, and I'd have to monitor them. I can't do that without access to a computer—I'd need to borrow one until I get my own back. People almost always get cocky and slip up, but it can take a while to become familiar enough with the patterns to see it happening."

Was he making an excuse? Was he trying to say *No, it's too hard*? It wasn't—it was actually quite within his capabilities, and if he had access to a computer, he could even use it to track his own.

He could get money for this, maybe enough to eke him out another month. Maybe enough to pay for the sheep, if that became necessary? There was literally no reason whatsoever to say no.

Except that he was afraid.

"We think he drove our friend to kill herself," Tegan urged, as though she could tell he was wavering. "And that he's only going to try again if he's not stopped."

Oh God, that was worse. What if he got it wrong? What if he couldn't find out who was doing this, and another child died and it was his fault?

"Please," said Maryam and reached across the table to close her hands over his as if she had strength to spare that she could lend him. "Take my computer now and track him down. Give me that piece of paper and I'll write down all my passwords. You've only got to find out who it is for us. We can make it stop. All right?"

The firm grip of her hands steadied his heart. The skewer in his back was only knitting-needle sized now, almost easy to live with. "All right," he agreed. "I'll see what I can do."

CHAPTER EIGHT

"It must be hard to deal with this," Sam said about a half an hour later, leaning back in his bench as if that would stop the vitriol from the computer screen from splashing into his face. Maryam had guided him through most of the incidents she could remember, and in lieu of his computer, he'd written down the dates and the platforms and the VP accounts on a sheet of her school notepaper.

"Yeah." Her lip wobbled, and Tegan slid closer to her, putting an arm around her back. More for warmth than for reassurance, probably. It really was getting very cold by now, two hours after the sun had gone down, and the day's pitiful warmth dissipated. "But, you know, you're the first one to say so."

Sam rubbed his solar plexus, which had begun to ache like a long-clenched fist. He was the wreck that he was partly from living too long in an atmosphere of outward cordiality and veiled backstabbing; he feared to think how much worse it would have been if the hatred had been overt. "I can't imagine anyone being treated with this level of hostility for so long not finding it hard."

He rubbed his eyes and looked at the weary, solemn faces around his table. It should have been peculiar to have them here, strangers in his refuge—in his fortress of solitude—but the truth was that below the surface, they were not so strange at all. They were a small nest of warm mice together under the floor of a house of terrifying giants.

"What is he even getting out of it?" Baffled, he reread the comment on her Tumblr that she had not wanted him to see—a long diatribe about Muslim men grooming young girls for sex, ending with *and you bet Osman Achmed knows more than he's saying. Has anyone investigated him? Maybe they should.*

"It's about my father," Maryam said, "I thank Allah he doesn't read my Tumblr. He hasn't seen it yet. But it will get out eventually. Someone will see it and tell him, and then what? My family have lived here two hundred years. We don't deserve this. I don't care that he calls me a slut or a cunt, but he can't say things about my father like that."

"And you've tried to get the comment taken down?"

"Of course." She brought her hand down flat on the table as if she was being very definite. "They did take it down, once. And then it went up again. If I take it down again, he'll know this is one that upsets me, and it'll get worse."

Between the sexual taunts and threats, the denigration and the deliberate blasphemy against her religion, and the sheer foaming hatred of some of the comments, after half an hour's exposure to this guy, Sam needed a bath and a stiff drink. He didn't want to imagine what it must be like for her to have it all wash over her relentlessly every time she switched the machine on to try to do her homework or talk to her friends. No single thing was unbearable, but cumulatively it was like being drowned in sewage.

He folded the screen down with a *click*, and some of the rigidity went out of everyone, as though an evil djinn had been put back in its lamp.

Ruan sighed and rubbed his nose. Tegan fidgeted, and Maryam rewound her scarf around her throat, pulling on a pair of fluffy pink gloves and her coat.

"You say he's doing it to others?" Sam asked. "Can you give me access to their accounts so I can see their comments too? They could screenshot everything and send me a file, but it would help to be able to see things happening in real time. Also, as I say, if you're getting repeated virus attacks, I'll need physical access to make sure they're clean, and you should keep a log of which sites *you* visit, who you talk to and when. Correlate that with if or when you get another attack. Even Skype can be used to install a virus on someone else's computer if you know how."

"I'll go back and get mine." Tegan stood. After dipping into her pocket for her phone to check the time, she gave Maryam a quick, lopsided smile that brought her resemblance to Ruan into high focus. "You want to come and have tea?"

"If your mam don't mind."

"Course she don't. We can do that coursework and print it out tonight." She looked over to Ruan. "Then I'll bring the laptop over to you first thing in the morning. Is that okay?"

Ruan was still leaning in the corner of the bench area, back against the wooden cladding of the wall, his scarf pulled up around his ears, one long leg resting crosswise over the other, ankle on knee. The scarf was black today, and with the black skinny jeans, black fingerless gloves, and black skiing coat, he looked like an off-piste Grim Reaper. A star shone out in the black tangle of his hair, somewhere in the angle of his jaw, and Sam's breath caught in wonder, though it was only an earring. Only the flash of the camping lantern on a single crystal earring.

"That's fine," Ruan said and gave Sam a frank smile. "I'll bring it up to you then." The shape of the smile changed briefly, as though he too had realized how strange it was, after the other night, that they were in this together. "Thanks for doing this," he said, letting a softness into the room with the words.

"Yeah, thanks, Mr. Atkins!"

"Cool van! See you."

The girls threw the back door open and scrambled out. A moment's fiddling with their mobiles later, and two wide beams of white light streamed out into the copse, picking out lichen, a cluster of red holly berries, and the tracks of the short path up to the road. They minced their way along the drying mud track until they came out onto the firmer pavement and flick of car lights of the main road. Then with a wave they were gone, down beyond the crest of the hill towards where Porthkennack's lights made a yellow smudge of the sky.

Ruan stayed. The air from the outside was actually warmer now than that within, and the day's wind had dried the dripping trees. Fading into the dark as he did, he might have been a spirit of the woods, a green man, or a fairy creature like the Black Knight who—according to the tourist brochure Sam had picked up at the service station— kennelled his sea serpents in the caves beneath Porthkennack's Caerdu Head. A genius loci with a soft, apologetic gaze.

"Listen. The business with the sheep? I'm sorry you come in for it. Auntie Jennifer, she wants someone to pay, you know? And no one can blame her for that. But it's not going to be you. I promise."

He might have been a faerie creature indeed. Something about his presence was larger than that of anyone Sam had encountered in the last year. It filled the back of the van and pressed on him with a weight like a down-filled duvet. A pressure it would have been comforting to give into, to draw all around himself and hide inside.

But that was probably just his own need to be rescued talking. He squirmed out from behind the table and instead of latching the door, he stepped out into the night. The warm expansiveness of Ruan's presence was better, less intimate in this setting, but now he had to do something to make his move outside look natural. "Do you think your auntie would mind if I lit a fire? I don't want to use up my gas bottle when there's wood all over the ground."

"I'll tell her I said you could." Ruan unfolded himself and reached for the kettle where it stood on the two-ring burner, like a man who'd never known what it was like not to feel at ease in company. "Shall I put teabags in mugs and bring them out?"

It wasn't pushy enough to feel like an imposition. Though Sam would normally have begrudged the loss of his peace, Ruan's assumption that they were friends now, that he was welcome, was quietly infectious. Watching the police rootle in his cupboards had been a kind of repeated static shock, but he didn't feel the need to watch Ruan, just cleared the biggest patch of dry ground he could find and lit a camp fire there, listening to doors open and close as though this happened all the time.

He was bending a notched stick over the fire to hold the kettle when Ruan returned with the cups, the last inch of milk in the bottle, and the heels of the loaf that had fed Sam for the last three days.

"There's toast in the making." He smiled, rolling a couple of larger logs out of their nests of fallen leaves and into the broadening warmth of the fire. "And I'll come by the One Stop in the morning and bring you groceries. You're clean out."

Sam wondered if he should object. If there was any pride left that would stand up and say *I don't need anyone's charity.* When all that came was thankfulness, he was glad to know there wasn't.

That was one of the things he had intended in taking up this itinerant life—to separate himself from pride over money.

"Thanks," he said instead, with the fire's warmth soothing away all the aches across the bridge of his nose that came with insufficient sleep. "I really don't have a lot of anything right now."

"So what's your story?" Ruan stretched out his long legs and crossed them at the ankles, watching tiny puffs of steam begin to wisp out of the mouth of the kettle. The afternoon's clouds had broken, and above the dome of golden firelight, above the cathedral arches of tree branches, the night was starred like his hair.

Don't. Don't fall for him just because he's the first person to take an interest in six months. He's still taking you to court, remember? And you can barely manage the issues you arrived with, let alone the strain of some kind of unrequited crush.

But he answered anyway, as if enchanted. "I used to work for my family's firm of investment advisers." He poured water on his tea and let the heat in his hands keep the memories safely distant. "We made obscene amounts of money and looked down at everyone who didn't. But . . ."

The light of the flames ran up and down Ruan's hands. Big bony hands, with prominent knuckles and smudges of colours between the first and second knuckle of the forefinger of the right hand. Once Sam had noticed how delicately they moved, restless in Ruan's hair and over his knees, he couldn't stop noticing.

"But I . . ." With such an audience, Sam wished he had a more dramatic tale to tell—some genuinely traumatic incident of swindling or bullying or dishonest conduct. As his parents often intimated, the truth was rather more pathetic. "Having all those people's savings in my hands. Knowing I was responsible if they lost value. It was . . ." The thought of it brought the old pain back, as though a ghost fist were squeezing his breastbone. The vertebrae of his spine grew hooks that caught at his lungs if he tried to breathe deep.

"It was just so terrifying. And the financial climate when you reach that level—high enough to know what the bankers and investors and market traders are actually doing with the money? Knowing that half the people you're interacting with are siphoning off funds into their own off-shore accounts? Knowing that you should do something about it—morally—but knowing that if you do, your family will never stop telling you what a disappointment you are until the end of time?" He shook his head, the tremor in his voice disgusting him, the well of condemnation in his stomach uncapped, and all the demons of self-reproach fighting among themselves to see who could shoulder out first.

"I couldn't eat or sleep. I tried antianxiety drugs, but I reacted badly to them and had to stop."

He reached down and combed his hands through the slimy leaf litter, hitting nettles and thorns and mud, reminding himself that his new life was cleaner. "My parents felt I was making a huge deal over nothing and I ought to just suck it up and be a man. Bad enough that I was gay without also being . . . *fragile*."

Though he'd broken it into pieces and offloaded as much of it as he could, shame still balanced like a boulder on his chest. "But they did send me to several therapists to try to make me more assertive."

Ruan laughed, fondly. "I'm guessing that didn't work."

"No." Sam smiled back. "Made it worse, in fact. Eventually I had a massive panic attack at work. I was sure I was dying. Then when the hospital told me there was nothing actually wrong with me? The shame. You've no idea! My family thought it was hilarious. They mocked me unmercifully for several months, and that was the point I knew I had to get out."

He steeled himself to look into Ruan's eyes, and found no matching contempt there, only the soft amber warmth of reflected firelight and a sympathetic interest he had rarely encountered before. None of the therapists had ever made him feel quite so listened to as this young Cornishman, and it made him smile again, the phantom heart pain easing up, everything inside him softening and smoothing out.

"Anyway," he continued. "I decided that the high-stress life was killing me. I sold my house and car and paid a man to equip the van with every modern convenience suitable for the road. Then I kept a couple of thousand pounds and gave the rest away—mostly paying back investors who had suffered by my advice."

Ruan would not understand why he had given away so much. Perhaps he was, as his parents thought, insane to do it, but he tried to explain anyway. "Money's a strange thing. When you have a lot of it, it begins to weigh on your thoughts all the time. Is it in the right place? Could it be earning more somewhere else? Will this risky investment fail? Am I being too timid, leaving it in a low-interest account? What if one of the banks goes bust? What if all of them do?" He shuddered. "I thought I would sleep better without it. Money isn't everything, you know?"

Ruan grimaced. "Well, I *don't*," he said. "Too much money's not a problem I've ever had. I wouldn't mind trying it. But I..." he hunched his shoulders as if a stray breeze had swung by specifically to blow ice down the back of his neck, "I wouldn't be without my family if that was what I had to pay for it. I'm luckier than you there, certain sure. Maybe it's time you had some luck of your own."

CHAPTER NINE

The idea followed Sam into sleep. Ruan had contemplatively drunk his tea, smiling at the fire for a short while after speaking, and then, perhaps to lighten the mood, he'd launched into a history of his drunken escapades at art college. Sam had laughed at the tale of his first tattoo, which even now Ruan didn't remember getting, and had started to ask if he could see it.

That had been when Ruan had decided it was time for him to go home, but the flustered sparkle of his eye and the thought that he was glad of Sam's presence had stuck with Sam as he ate the last remnants of his toast, tried to drown out the gnawing of hunger with watery hot chocolate, and went to bed.

He'd dreamed of a fox snuffling around his van, its russet fur flattened in the gust of the winter wind. In the dream, he had ignored it—wild beasts were better left outside. He'd drawn the unfamiliar duvet up over his shoulder and turned his back on it. The next thing he knew, a cold nose was pushed into his cheek. He came to sudden wakefulness looking up the long slope of a whiskered snout into curious, concerned eyes. And then he'd woken up a second time, for real, and found a spot of condensation had dripped from the roof onto his face.

Another chilled the crown of his head as he swung up into a sitting position and blearily reached to switch on Maryam's laptop. The wind-turbine had charged both the laptop and his phone overnight—a good result given that it was overshadowed by trees. He intended to have a quick look to see if there were any new messages before he raked up the fire outside and drank the last spoonful of his coffee with the last of his hot chocolate. But the fire was sidelined when he found that there had been two new messages on Facebook, three on Twitter, and a slew on Tumblr. Also the programme he had written to try to trace back their VPN addresses to their original had compiled overnight and was ready to run.

He pulled his feet back into the warmth, dragged the computer into his lap, and grabbed for the pen and half notebook Maryam had left him, to analyse the syntax of the messages. There were verbal tricks that they shared—already he was fairly sure all the messages were coming from a single person, but he was less certain they were coming from a single computer.

That was perhaps not surprising—everyone had a PC and a laptop and a phone these days. A single-originating bastard might have two or three devices from which to spread his poison.

Having got a jump on starting while he was still too sleepy to feel the weight of the responsibility of the task, Sam was soon diverted by the sheer intricacy of the puzzle—by working out how everything fitted together. It was better than crosswords! But while he was at it, he also initialized the programme he'd written to find his MacBook. If it was on, it should be broadcasting its own location, waiting for him to come and bring it home . . .

Knock, knock.

"I brought breakfast!"

He'd forgotten that Ruan was coming back. Something inside him rose and broke the surface like the long swell of the back of a whale. How odd it was to hear another human voice interrupting his solitude and not to resent it. How odd, but not at all unwelcome.

"Hold on," he shouted. "I'm not dressed."

"Oh, I don't mind at all."

A light voice. He'd begun to realize that the hint of laughter was native to it—that the hushed and sober tones he'd heard in it at first were unusual. It made his own face twitch into a smile as if by remote control.

You're not falling for him, remember? But he was too flustered to remember the reasons why not. This time, he only bothered to shimmy into trousers before opening the door, and found Ruan once more in his rainbow woollens, with two plastic carrier bags in his hands and a *Death Note* rucksack perched precariously over one shoulder.

Apparently Ruan didn't have a day job either. Nor must he have any kind of social filter over his nosiness, because he'd already swept the whole van with a curious gaze that was now lingering appreciatively on Sam's shoulders, bare beneath his white vest.

"Hello," Sam said, while a long-lost warmth welled out of his chest and set his cheeks aflame. He'd forgotten how to deal with this—had never actually tried picking people up while sober. The prospect had always been too terrifying. *And, besides, you're not in the market for a relationship, remember?* He jammed his hands into the arms of a T-shirt and pulled it defensively over his head. "I'm sorry. I forgot you were coming."

"I suppose there's no call to wake up early in a place like yours." Ruan stepped inside without being invited and began opening cupboards and putting groceries away. "My mam gets the whole house up at half six, and you got to be quick to the bathroom or there's no chance of a shower. Then there's Jimmy and Lora to get to school, and Mam and Da to get to work. And they're all making their lunches in the meantime. I've come up here for a bit of peace."

Sam was reminded of the fox—it was as if he'd been adopted, almost against his will, by a denizen of the copse. He might have resented it more if it hadn't been done with such sunny goodwill, and had not come with jars of coffee and cartons of tea, with milk and bread and cans of beans. That wasn't breakfast. That was a week's groceries, another week of not having either to work or starve.

He was struggling with the right words of gratitude when Ruan jumped back down, leaving the door to flap open behind him. "There's some warmth left in this fire. I'll see if I can rake it up and put the kettle on. Tegan's laptop's in the bag there."

Sam transferred his IP tracking programme from Maryam's to Tegan's and then brought them outside to sit on a tussock each, while he bent and pegged down some branches, rigging his green tarpaulin over the top to make a windbreak-cum-shelter around the fire. Ruan had the embers raked together already, and was crumpling an old newspaper to serve as kindling. "There's dry wood in the passenger footwell," Sam said with another surge of mingled affection and disbelief. How was this happening? *Was* it really happening at all? "If you want good stuff to burn."

Since the dry wood was being used, he spent ten minutes stepping through the tangles of the copse, picking up wet fallen branches to replace it with, and by the time he returned, the fire was crackling, the area behind the windbreak was actually warm, and Ruan had discovered Sam's frying pan and was cooking bacon over the flames. The smell of wood-smoke and fat, acrid, salty, and savoury, was a punch in the throat and the heart alike, as the blue vapour of the steaming kettle rose against a beaming blue sky.

Sam had been running away from pain so long he'd forgotten there was something on the other side of it. He'd forgotten that joy was a thing, and it edged back into his life as though scared it was going to be turned away.

As he poured water into the mugs of coffee, the bright red of a flashing box on Maryam's computer caught the corner of his eye. After several failed attempts—telling in itself because it was rare that his laptop was out of satellite range—his tracking programme had finally located his MacBook. "Yes!" He grinned, taking a celebratory sip of coffee, feeling it burn the back of his throat as a weirdly happy high note. "Got you, you bastard."

"I thought you said it was going to take a long time?" Ruan forked a couple of rashers of crisp brown bacon onto bread and butter and passed it to him with an expression that wasn't quite as pleased as Sam had hoped. Almost instantly, his shy new happiness vanished. What was that about? Had he done something wrong?

"Oh, I'm sorry," he said, taking a bite of bacon sandwich, and closing his eyes as the sleek satisfaction of warm fat filled his unaccustomed mouth. "I didn't mean I'd got the person who's been sending the messages. I meant I'd got the person who stole my computer. The other thing will take longer, but I have specialized software on my MacBook, so getting it back will help."

The advice of his therapist warred with his instincts inside him. Instinct wanted to go, look, right now. Therapy told him to be mindful of enjoying his sandwich first.

But why wait? The bacon was joy, and the flutter of Ruan's crow-black, feather-soft hair around his plush mouth was joy. Why wouldn't having the location of his lost everything just augment the moment, make it better?

Swallowing the rest of his breakfast without tasting it, he sat on "his" tree stump and lifted the laptop onto his knee, squinting at the letters on the backlit screen—trying to pick them out in the brightness of the morning sky.

In an attempt to see clearly, he closed up the social media programmes, glad to unclutter the screen and remove the ugliness of their threats. Then he brought up the window with his tracking code. It had already resolved into a string of coordinates. Yes! Sometimes he almost believed he could achieve things—almost believed he could get things right. And how wonderful to be able to do it with Ruan watching. He wanted—with a strength that startled him. For the first time in years he wanted something beyond mere survival and peace. He wanted Ruan to look at him and find him good.

"Now I just copy this into Google Maps, and we should be staring down at this bastard's house."

He cut and pasted, watched the map narrow in. The shape of the peninsula on which Porthkennack was built was instantly recognisable, the little rounded arrow of *You are here* hovering over the east coast.

A suspicious lack of built-up areas met his eye, added punishing weights to his sense of victory. He switched to street view just to be sure, swirling dizzyingly through a three-sixty blur of empty field. Grass and gorse. A clump of wool hanging from a barbed wire fence. All the new strength went out of his back at once, and he became aware of the permanent ache that had settled like the stumps of sawn-off wings just beneath his shoulder blades.

"It's somewhere near the Angel and Eagle pub," he said, dully. "On the headland there. But there's no building, not even a shed. He must have found the tracker and tossed it out."

The sheer futility of existence overwhelmed Sam briefly, like being sucked into quicksand. Why did he bother trying when he never succeeded in anything and never would?

A glance at Ruan was strengthening though—the long, lanky shape of him and the sense that whatever this failure was, he was not alone in it for once. He scraped up his hope with mental fingernails.

"I suppose the signal could have come from inside a car, and it drove away before we looked. I can't think why he'd leave the laptop in the middle of the field. I'll wait ten minutes and see if the coordinates have changed. If they have, then he's in a car. He'll have to go home at some point, and I can set the police on him then."

"That must be it," Ruan agreed slowly, his gaze cast down. "In a car, certain sure." His voice had lost all of its lightness, and when he looked up, those starry eyes of his were steel shutters. The thought that he had seen something in the field that Sam had not—something that concerned and distressed him—presented itself to Sam forcefully. But then Sam so often thought fanciful and untrue things, that he could hardly trust his perception with this.

Ruan scrambled to his feet. "Well, I'd better be off. I promised I'd help Mam with the lunch rush at the chippy, and I'm cutting it fine already."

The trouble with paranoia, Sam thought as he watched Ruan backpedal from the fireside, then turn and almost run down the hill and away, was that sometimes they really were out to get you. He might be prone to panic, prone to fear the irrational worst. But whatever had just happened there—that wasn't normal, was it? He wasn't completely irrational, was he, to think that something was going on, and Ruan was definitely not his easy self about it?

CHAPTER
TEN

"That's two breakfast specials, a coffee, and a tea?" Ruan's mam was saying to the customers on table three as he came in. She tucked her notebook and pen back in the pocket of her lace-trimmed black apron, and nodded to him with a sharpening of her eyes that said, *Trouble?*

He followed her behind the counter, where Tegan's sister Marie was bringing two plates of ham, egg, and chips out of the kitchen, and Da was hollering from the fish fryer that there was someone at the ice cream window demanding a ninety-nine. Ruan stepped up to the window automatically and slid it open, letting piercing sea air through to settle like dry ice around everyone's feet.

Outside stood one of those hearty families—ten-year-old and father in wetsuits with wet hair, determined that a seaside holiday should involve ice cream even if it was the middle of December. Mother and teenage daughter huddled in every towel they owned, shivering and asking for hot chocolate. When he had served them and relatched the window, his mam was back from running the drinks out to table three.

"Hello, love. I didn't expect you so early," she said, tucking a spiral of coppery hair back into the mob cap of her uniform. "One of them jobs that always takes an age, in my experience—mending computers."

The hair had started life as black as his own, but when she had found her first grey streak she decided that if she was going to have to dye it anyway, she might as well have some fun with it. Last year she'd been blonde. It was anyone's guess what next month would bring. The purple had been surprisingly good, but the green had looked too much like an angry mermaid and had frightened the customers.

"Well, he hasn't finished yet," Ruan admitted, and at his father's hand signal, he tugged an apron out of the linen drawer and took over the hot plates. "But I . . . ah. I wanted to ask you something."

"Oh yeah?" she said, faintly lilting, as if she could already tell this was an affair of the heart. Except that it wasn't, of course. "Give me a minute."

She dived out again into the restaurant, circling around, giving the tables—black, decorated with faux newspaper print and red edgings—a quick wipe down, zeroing in on table four, who were sipping their drinks and had put their menus down as though they had finally made up their minds. While he was waiting for her to return, Ruan fried eggs, bacon, hash browns, and mushrooms for the all-day-breakfast order, trying not to allow the smell of the bacon to send him back to Foxglove Copse.

"One cod and chips, one scampi and chips, and a chip butty." Mam called out the new order as she returned, and he jotted it down on the pad. "What was it you wanted to ask, love?"

"Suppose someone had had something stolen." Ruan sidled up to the problem as tactfully as he could. In the back of his mind, he was remembering Sam Atkins crouched by a silver birch with his face pressed to the bark like he had no other living thing to give him comfort. It always did give Ruan a kind of anger and a kind of ache to watch anyone suffering and not to do anything about it. "And someone else had a good idea where it might be. D'you think that person ought to go and get it back?"

A terrible lemon-sharp light sliced from the ice cream window, sun on the sea. It picked out the wrinkles and dry paperiness of his mam's skin under that wealth of penny-bright hair, and briefly she looked like she'd seen far too much in her life.

"You don't need me to say yes to that." She leaned carefully against the chilled desserts cabinet. "Of course they should. Unless there was something else you weren't telling me about. How about you start again without the mystery and tell me what you actually mean?"

Ruan dished the fried food onto plates and passed them to Marie, who ladled on beans and two slices of toast and carried them out. He wondered how much Mam had heard from Jennifer and the neighbours. How much she had deduced from his own behaviour. He settled on *everything*.

"Well, you know this lad who's camped up on Jennifer's land, Jennifer's accused of killing one of her sheep?"

"With witchcraft, no less," she agreed. "Yeah, I heard."

"His name's Sam." Ruan bent over the hot plate, scraping off any bits of leftover food before they could burn, uncertain whether the heat on his face was from the cooker or his own blush. "And Jennifer herself don't honestly think he did it."

"Is that so?" she said. "Cause I thought she seemed sure enough."

"I'm . . ." Sam came bright into his mind, as he had been doing with increasing frequency all day. Sandy, badly cut hair and a beard that was a suggestion of gilding around his lips. Pink lips, and Scandinavian cheekbones, and blue eyes, as pale and as near-transparent as the flame of a lighter. Beauty, yes, but something more than that. He was tall, but so thin—he'd be handsomer if the bones of his face weren't so clearly visible, and if his expression wasn't that of the world's sin-eater. Like someone who knew they'd done no wrong but knew it was theirs to take the punishment regardless.

The man just had a face that screamed *innocent* at Ruan, *innocent and falsely accused.*

Even though he was the very man we found crouched over a dead sheep's head, like he was fiddling with the pentagram he already knew more about than anyone else I've ever met?

"I'm . . . mostly sure, myself."

The two occupied tables now had their orders. Unlike the summer, when there wouldn't be a lull from May to September, there was time for them all to have a coffee, and for Da to slip out onto the seafront for a cigarette.

"Anyway," Ruan started again, remembering that he had not told Mam about the bullying, because it would only worry her and he was handling it. "Like I said, he said he was some kind of tech guru, so I took Tegan's laptop up there to see if he could debug it, and he's running some stuff on that now. But he asked if he could use it to track his own MacBook that was stolen while we were talking to him about the sheep, and I said yes."

"Mm-hmm?"

"Well, he tracked it to a field just outside the Angel."

She had been stirring one white and one brown sugar into her coffee. Her spoon came to rest with a sudden *clink*. "Oh yes?" she said, but she'd clearly caught on.

"He thought maybe it was in a car that had moved on, but what I thought was that . . ."

"Ruan . . ."

"I thought that maybe it was in the caves underneath."

Mam put one hand across her forehead like she was holding in a headache or an apprehension. "Oh Ruan. Leave it. What goes on down there in those caves? That's Lusmoore business. You don't want to go stirring that up for the sake of some outsider, especially one that's already in trouble with the police. Haven't we told you often enough not to have nothing to do with the Lusmoores, if you know what's good for you? Leave it, all right? For my sake and your own."

There were things you didn't say outright about your neighbours, and his mother's hints were all the more sinister for being so vague, delivered in such a hushed and urgent tone, as though the very stones beneath their feet were listening in. Ever since he'd been a tiny child, the whole town had talked about the Lusmoores the same way they talked about the fair folk—as creatures whose wrong side you didn't want to be on. And yet they were normal folk like everyone else, weren't they? They might operate a little outside the law, like Cornish smugglers always had, but they couldn't really deserve this amount of awe and terror.

"It's my lifeline." Sam's words came back to him plaintively, and Sam was so clearly barely hanging on the end of that line. No matter how suspicious Sam's appearance on the scene of the crime might be, no one could say he'd faked the starvation tightness of the skin over his bones, or the trembling that had gone in long sweeps down his back as he fought himself for control, fought himself to stop panicking, wanting to run away. He was like a wild thing himself. There'd been many a moment of tension between them when Ruan felt sure if he made too sudden a move the other man would spook and flee away like a startled deer.

"It's my lifeline."

"You don't really need me here do you?" Ruan said, as the clock in the kitchen flicked over to 14:00.

Her lips quirked. "I'm always glad to see you, though. How's the job hunting? Anything yet?"

He hadn't thought about it this week, but then it was only Monday. "Not yet. It's early days, though."

With a wave, he ducked back out of the steamy warmth of the café. Wrapping his scarf three times around his neck and face, he turned his collar up and began the uphill slog towards the town centre. Yesterday's rain had washed the streets which now shone bright and bleak between closed shops. Ropes denuded of flags battered their poles. Unlit Christmas lights creaked against supports that in warmer months bore overflowing baskets of flowers.

Ruan walked up to the neat, new-built housing estate that had taken away half of Bandry Park, where a carefully arranged palate of yellow houses had not yet had time to mellow into place. He stopped outside the pristine bungalow in the centre of it all, where Wyn Lusmoore—known as Grandma Wyn to the locals—presided over her notorious clan. Electric gates barred his entrance. Sensors on the gate and cameras beneath the roof eves blinked with little red lights. In the garden, an enormous inflatable Santa was fighting a losing battle against the wind, being battered back and forth between a shed done up as a nativity scene, and an LED wonderland whose light display grew more spectacular every year.

In the summer there were gnomes.

Ruan took a deep breath, aware that he was entering into the lair of the beast, but still convinced that his parents and neighbours were making a big deal out of nothing. All the hushed voices and the ancestral disapproval and nothing but rumour and gossip at the bottom of it. He pressed the gate buzzer. "It's Ruan? Ruan Gwynn? I wanted to speak to Grandma Wyn."

Silently, the gate opened by itself, passing within an inch of Wyn's brand-new shiny Mini. Not a weed met his foot as he walked down the crazy paving, across a lawn of perfect stripes, and the front door too opened for him by itself without him needing to knock.

They said if you smiled, it fooled your brain into being happy, right? Ruan pasted on a grin and leaned over the threshold. "Hello?"

"Just come straight in," Grandma Wyn herself shouted back. "I'm in the kitchen."

It was a voice that he'd heard for many years behind a microphone at St. Ia's church fete, judging the cakes and jams. Being nervous of it seemed stupid. And yet, with his mother's urgent warning still fresh in his mind, he was. Grandma Wyn was the unacknowledged matriarch of the Lusmoore clan, and *we don't talk about the Lusmoores. If we know what's good for us, we don't have nothing to do with the Lusmoores.*

Why was he defying that constant refrain? Just for some outsider with a flickering shy blue gaze and no one else to stand by him? He must be mad.

To be extra tactful, Ruan took his shoes off before stepping over the threshold onto the deep softness of the pure-white carpet. Again as it often did in the afternoon, the sky had clouded over as he walked, and the hall was in gloom. Night was already making its approach known, and it was random curiosity when he glanced into the living room—he only wanted to know if she really had a Jacuzzi in the middle of the floor, like Jimmy said.

No evidence of a Jacuzzi, but an open laptop sat on the marble coffee table. Its back was towards him, but its lit screen reflected in the dark windows, and was . . . not as interesting as he'd hoped. Just a plan of a large holiday camp and some maths that was perhaps projections of how much money it might bring in. Boring. He had been hoping for something a little more James Bond—plans for a doomsday machine, perhaps.

His smile relaxed as he passed hurriedly by and came to the kitchen, where Grandma Wyn was elbow-deep in crumble topping. She had the figure of a woman who liked her food, grey-streaked black hair and black-coffee eyes in a round, high-coloured face. Her powerful forearms were all over flour, and a scent of apple and cinnamon rose like a benediction from a pan on the stove beside her.

Clever eyes. They flicked up to catch his gaze as he entered the room, and he froze like a cat spritzed with water.

"Ruan Gwynn," she repeated, her tone kindly and interested, somewhere between grandmotherly and school-ma'am. "Well, I haven't seen a Gwynn here since I had to help your great-uncle Connor with a bit of an embarrassment— But we won't talk about that. What can I do for you?"

CHAPTER ELEVEN

In her pristine kitchen, full of the warmth of a preheated oven, and the glister from the stainless steel tops of the workbenches, the thought of using the word *theft* seemed plain rude.

"Friend of mine's lost his computer," he managed, watching the thick slices of apple in the pan begin to disintegrate into sauce—a lava-like gloop as slow bubbles rose to the surface.

"Right so?" She gave the crumble one last stir, sifting the fine particles through her fingers, like someone who has no particular interest in the subject and is waiting for it to become relevant. "Put the kettle on, will you? I don't want to touch it with these hands."

Oh God, what was he doing here? She ran the Women's Institute, and she always dressed up in Cornish traditional dress for the institute's eisteddfod, and she'd raised such a brood of sons and grandkids. The last thing she needed was for some tosser like him—university educated, no less, thinks he's better than everyone—to come sniffing round her state-of-the-art kitchen and accusing her of . . . something.

That didn't mean he wasn't going to take the chance to open a few cupboards in the guise of looking for the tea bags. His mam would be interested to know what kind of good china she used.

Ruan lifted the prettily enamelled kettle from its base and went to fill it at the sink, only for Grandma Wyn to shoulder him aside and make him wait as she washed the flour and fat mixture from her fingers. A scent of floral perfume and a whiff of sweat met his nose, and he didn't know if he was being taught that she was soft but immovable, or if he was still trying to read too many spy films into the situation.

He was still glad when he could move away though, setting the full kettle back on its base to boil.

"Right." She wiped her hands dry on a tea towel and gestured him to a seat at the oak settle. "What was it about this computer?"

"My friend has some kind of a chip in it, or a programme or something—I didn't follow that bit. Like a tracking device."

She leaned forward encouragingly with her plump hands folded over her *Kiss the cook* apron. He'd expected a reaction, a flinch, perhaps, but her calmness gave him the creeps.

"Oh yes?"

"Well." Ruan didn't have her poise. He dampened his lips with his tongue and grasped the table like the edge of a cliff. "Well, it said his laptop was in the caves under the Angel."

Still nothing. He felt like a bird pinned beneath a cat's unmoving stare. "And I knew that was Lusmoore territory."

The click of the kettle switching itself off made all the blood in him jump a foot in the air. Fortunately not visibly. Wyn got up like the surge of an iceberg over a high wave and turned her back on him to pour water into mugs. Ruan felt he had been judged not good enough for the teapot and the cups.

"We have some warehouses under there, certain sure." She stirred milk into the mugs ponderingly. "I still don't know what you're saying to me, though."

Oh, but maybe it really was Bond-like, this delicate game of manners and bluff. Ruan smiled at her as she turned to place the tea in front of him. "My friend wanted to go to the police and get them to find it for him. I said there wasn't any reason to involve the police. I'd just come and ask you."

Grandma Wyn's shoulders dropped with an air of relief, as though she had been expecting something worse, and she rose to her feet again to bring out an earthenware biscuit barrel and offer him a choice of homemade Viennese whirl or a fondant fancy.

"That was considerate of you." She returned the smile as he bit too hard into the fondant fancy and bright cerise icing burst to release an explosion of cherry-flavoured buttercream into his unprepared mouth. "They do break things, the police. Terrible clumsy they are."

She snapped her Viennese whirl into several pieces and ate one with ostentatious neatness while he rinsed the cloying sweetness of buttercream out of his mouth with tea. "And they get everyone aflutter. Much better to come to me. Well now." Neatly but quickly, she downed the rest of the biscuit and her own drink. Then she rose and opened a hatch to what might be the dining room or an office beyond.

"Martin! Harry!"

The dining room door and the door out into the hall, from which he'd come, opened within seconds of each other as two burly men came through. Instinctively, Ruan pressed himself against the back of his seat. Something about the way they walked set off ancient alarms in his hind brain.

"This is my grandson Harry." Wyn's smile was a potent combination of pride and one-upmanship. Harry with his bleached-blond hair and salon tan seemed to be doing quite well for himself, if his gold sovereign rings and necklace could be believed. "And my nan's sister's boy, Martin."

Martin was older. His white hair and weathered, ruddy cheeks gave him the appearance of a kindly ship's captain, but the tattoos on his knuckles were stick-and-poke jobs, typical of prison, blurred and blue like a curse slurred out drunkenly in the dark. The two men were very different from one another, but they shared a flatness of eye that Ruan associated more with sharks than humans—a lack of inward reflection, of conscience.

Ruan grimaced a continuing smile and tried not to seem as petrified as he suddenly felt. "Hi."

They didn't smile back, but Wyn did, easing the atmosphere down from imminent death to mere unspoken threat. "You know we own quite a few antique and secondhand shops?" She put her hand under Ruan's elbow, urging him to stand up. He rose and stood still while she fussed over rewrapping his scarf and drawing his woolly hat over his hair in a way that might look tender but felt like he was a chicken being dressed for the butcher's slab. A lifetime of vague warnings combined with a vivid imagination to suggest that he had properly run his head into the noose now. He had marched into Mafia headquarters and would be lucky to get out alive.

"We're always buying new stock for 'em. Sometimes people will cheat us by trying to pass on to us goods that have been stolen. Well, we've no use for that. If there's a stolen laptop on our premises, I'm glad to have the opportunity to return it to its owner free of charge, no matter what I had to spend to buy it. The boys here will take you, make sure you don't get lost on the way."

She tucked his hair under the rim of his hat, while he tried not to flinch at the invasion of his personal space. "Give my regards to your mother," she finished. "And you can tell your friend he's no need of the police. The Lusmoores are as honest as the day is long."

"Come on, then." Martin gave a jerk of the chin, and Ruan went after him as though pulled. He had to sit down on the floor in the hall to put on his shoes—his knees too wobbly to balance on one foot. After which, he expected to go out into the front garden, where the many coloured Christmas lights were already strobing through the fan window of the front door.

But they led him through the sitting room instead to a square little room beside the downstairs toilet. A hatch in the floor there opened into a cellar stairway, steep as a shipboard ladder. A bare, waterproof bulb snapped on as Harry came in behind them. Ruan was squashed in the tiny room between them, his sense of himself abraded by their rough presence. He didn't want to go down the hole, into the dark.

"In you get," said Harry. "Don't be worried about no dragons. We haven't seen them around for years, have we Marty?"

Dragons were currently the last thing on Ruan's mind. *They tried to spare me this—all those friends and neighbours who warned me away.* They'd had their own experiences of this or worse, and that was what lay behind the warnings.

But Porthkennack's native families knew what was due to each of them. Perhaps the smuggling business required an occasional snitch to vanish. Maybe a tourist or two who saw something they shouldn't've was frightened away or worse. But the Lusmoores must know that they could threaten Ruan all they liked, but that unspoken social contract not to meddle in the Lusmoores' business as long as they kept themselves to themselves would not survive them hurting him. There was a hell of a lot the locals could tell the police about them if a Gwynn came to harm at their hands.

He took a deep, steadying breath, turned, and went down backwards like a sailor into the belly of a ship. With every step, the chill and the damp bit deeper, and the knowledge of dark—if that light was snapped off and the hatch lowered—hunkered over him like a monster with its prey. What if they did just that? What if they shut the door, put out the light, and left him? He hadn't told anyone where he was going.

Terror numbed his fingers and set his backbone aquiver as if he'd been doused in ice water. Sam would come for him. Maybe not himself—Ruan couldn't imagine a man as paralysed with nerves as Sam going through with some rescuing-hero crap—but he would figure it out. He would send the police.

Ruan's corpse could be five miles out to sea by then, with nothing at all to link Wyn or her boys to his death. If they couldn't prove responsibility, the locals wouldn't do anything—other than mutter a bit louder, try to terrify their kids into obedience even more.

Martin's boot clanked onto the step as Ruan reached the ground. He threaded his hands up his coat sleeves and warmed them in the crook of his elbows as an excuse to hug himself. Telling himself to stop imagining the worst, he watched "the boys" come down with a glimmering of relief.

"This way, then." Martin led them through a small, dusty cellar half filled with wine racks and old broken furniture to a narrow door in the left-hand corner. It opened on an unromantic concrete corridor going straight out, southeast. A newly dug, newly poured smell clung to it as though there were still particles of powder in the air.

Ruan didn't know how long he walked after that—it felt like hours before he thought to check his watch, but after passing three or four padlocked doors on each side, the concrete ended and they stepped out of the light onto rough stone.

"You be careful now." Martin put a crushing grip on his shoulder. "This bit's tricky underfoot. Slippery sometimes too. You keep your mind on that and not on where you're going, all right?"

"Honest as the day is long." And it was the winter, when the day lasted seven hours out of twenty-four. Ruan shivered again and nodded in the light of Martin's torch.

"What's your friend's laptop like?" Harry asked, as they scrambled up an incline with a great emptiness and echo around them—the torches didn't penetrate far enough to show any walls, but in the distance it really did sound like something huge was sleeping, its cold breath sighing in and out.

Probably the sea.

"It's a MacBook Pro? It would have been brought in three nights ago, or the day after, I suppose."

"Ah, right." Harry was behind him—he couldn't read the man's features, but he heard a kind of worldly amusement in the tone that said *typical.* "I think I know the one."

"Do you know who brought it in?" Ruan asked, greatly daring, because the chances were that whoever had stolen the laptop had killed the sheep too. Chances were it was a Lusmoore, unless of course the witch had just sold the laptop to the nearest convenient Lusmoore at the closest pub. But he'd get nowhere if he said so—they had strong stomachs for the kind of behaviour they would tolerate from family members, and even if they did know who was doing this, they would never tell.

"No, I don't." Harry's mouth snapped shut like a clam, and the semifriendly banter of the journey came to an abrupt end. Ruan wobbled over the final stone bridge and up into narrower passages. The twisting stairs, the sighing in the dark, and the swirling of two torch spots had begun to dizzy him. His legs ached, and right behind his spine there itched a continual warning that he could disappear down here and never see the sun again.

It was still another twenty minutes before they ushered him into a larger cellar, whose shelves were stacked with boxes, where they then shoved the impossibly tiny white rectangle of a MacBook into his hands. He almost dropped it. Its shut case was covered with a skin of purple, white, and gold that depicted an angel holding in one hand a flaming sword and in the other a shield so large that it brushed the creature's toes and their chin. On the shield, in strokes of midnight blue, a pentagram stood out like a branding iron, surrounded by flames.

"Someone's into some creepy shit, eh?" Harry nudged him, lips drawing up just enough to show a sliver of nicotine-stained teeth in what was evidently meant to be a comradely smile.

Ruan wanted to be able to say, *Just 'cause you're ignorant doesn't mean it's bad. I know the guy, and you're a lot scarier than he is,* but self-preservation held him back. Even if he did want to talk about it, it certainly wouldn't be to them. "I don't know. I think it's pretty metal."

"Kids," Martin scoffed, but he put a hand on Ruan's shoulder and pushed him towards a distant stair. "You go up there. Right, then left. You'll come out in the Angel. You can get a cab home or walk from there."

CHAPTER TWELVE

On the long walk back up the spine of the peninsula towards Auntie Jennifer's farm, Ruan found himself feeling mythical. He'd been down into the underworld, and he'd come away with the prize. As he passed the last house on the edge of town (the Sandersons' house, with the Dobermann and all that dark twisted topiary), the sun began to lower into a faintly warm sunset. Clouds stroked bars of burning rose and orange over a flood of heavy golden light. The houses gave way to farmland and the hummocks of the Stone Age, and he felt like he should be accompanied by soft metal, wailing guitars. The young hero, having passed his first test, returning for the praise of his . . .

Master? Mentor? Nah. Neither of those fitted Sam Atkins. He wasn't sure what did, still kind of off-centre about the pentagram on the computer in his hand. His knee-jerk reaction was to associate them with horror movies on one hand and now with dead sheep. But Sam had looked even at the symbol as though it was a writing in another language. Not an automatic portal for demons to come through, but some kind of puzzle or tool. Maybe they were like most things, and you could use them for good or for bad, depending on what good or evil was inside you?

He wished he could shut up the little niggle that said, *That's as maybe, or maybe it's some Friday the thirteenth shit*, but he couldn't, so he'd do the next best thing and watch Sam, get to know him. Eventually the truth would come out, right? Like the man said himself, even the most cunning deceiver must slip up eventually. In the meantime, Ruan would be sensibly wary. He'd take his mam's advice and back off, protect himself, not go rushing into things like some roleplay paladin, sure his own righteousness would protect him.

Yep. He nodded as he swung over the stile that let foot travellers onto Jennifer's land, through the barbed wire fence. He'd be clever this time and hold back his trust until he was sure its potential recipient deserved it. He'd take a leaf out of Jennifer's book and fence in what was his with barbed wire, like it wasn't already too late to protect it.

Jennifer's farm stretched from one side of the headland to the other, fresh and green. In the winter there was a wind-scoured freedom to it, as the great waves tossed and spumed around it among the deadly rocks. The main road to and from Porthkennack pierced Jennifer's land in two, bordered with orange crocosmia flowers and poppies and white Michaelmas daisies, but the farm itself was Porthkennack's limit on the southern side, as the sea was north, east, and west. The town had nowhere left to grow into. It would have to stay itself—big enough for novelty but small enough so he could know practically everyone that lived there regular.

Ruan liked it that way.

The long shadows of the trees of Foxglove Copse touched him first as he came up the hill, sun behind the trunks and glittering through in brassy, boiling stripes. He took a deep breath to let his decision settle into his bones. He'd been hospitable, he'd got Sam's computer back for him, and now he was free of the obligation to protect the other man. He was going to protect himself. At least until he was sure.

Sky and sun glittered on the surface of the small brook that meandered out of the copse, a ribbon of heavenly radiance bisecting the darkening fields. Ruan hopped over it and went on up. The wind fell as he came into the shelter of the trees, and in the calm, the ghost of warmth drew fleeting scents of sap and sleeping earth out of the wood. The sun was right down on the horizon now, shining straight at him, and going into the trees was like walking into a hall whose pillars were of golden flame.

Part of him even then noticed the design—the stark beauty of black trunks and bare branches against the silent roar of the radiance. He was going to have to put that somewhere on himself—left inner arm or calf or thigh. The thought of the high, thin pain of the needle, the scrape and burn of the newly completed tattoo, inflamed and sensitive, boiled up him like the light, made his breath catch in something halfway between arousal and awe.

So he was already primed when he pushed past the ball of mistletoe on the oak next to Sam's van and stopped there as if struck. Sam had parked next to the stream, but the windbreak of the little campsite screened off the van, and for that first long moment they might have been right back in the Stone Age, or further, into legend, because Sam had taken off all his clothes bar a pair of blue boxers, and he was bathing—sitting in the cold little rivulet with that wall of sun gilding his back, his cupped hands full of water and flame that glittered as he poured them over his hair.

Ruan froze in place. Didn't make a sound, though his heart raced with heat and shame. He was trespassing, but he didn't intend to leave.

Water rolled from Sam's darkened hair and beaded on his pale eyelashes. With his eyes closed, thinking himself alone, his expression was soft, unguarded—the expression of someone who is lost and isn't even going to try calling out for help, because they know no one will come.

There were cold hollows between each of his ribs and over his collarbones. He'd probably always been slenderly built, but now he looked ethereal and painful, like one of the plague ghosts that were said to appear on misty afternoons in Bandry Park.

Ruan wanted to draw him, or to press his own fingers and tongue in all the hollows where Sam had been starved, and tease out warmth and fullness from him. He smiled at his own self-delusion. Distance? Wariness? Waiting? Who had he thought he was fooling? None of those things were anywhere in his character. He was going to rush into this like he always did, and survive it or not as it came.

Not a mentor, certain sure. Something stranger than that, chancy and uncertain, elvish maybe, and therein lay the enchantment.

"You must be fucking freezing," Ruan's mouth said without his permission. Sam's eyes flew open as he jumped backwards. One hand went behind him for support, slid on a mossy stone, and he toppled over into the water. It closed over his face briefly, before he was surging out again, coughing with a wheezy constricted noise that Ruan didn't like at all. Ruan went for the van, reassured a little by the fact that, once he got into the camp clearing properly, he found the fire was lit and a towel draped over a branch near it to warm. He grabbed it and held it out.

Sam was now on his feet, with one arm wrapped around himself and the other hand placed across his mouth as if holding in a scream. It seemed he was contemplating fleeing, as he stood looking over Ruan's shoulder. And then his pellucid blue eyes slid to Ruan's and whatever he saw there must have reassured him. He reached out and took the towel, slipped it around suddenly shivering shoulders.

"I'm sorry." Ruan smiled. "I should have made some noise coming up. I didn't mean to startle you."

"It's . . . um. It's fine." Sam gave a jerk of a nod and stepped away from him, towelling down his hair as an obvious excuse to look aside.

Ruan followed him to the campsite, watched him sidle up close to the fire and stand over it, soaking up its warmth. *I'm going to look after you now*, he thought, but didn't say.

"Isn't it too cold for bathing in streams, though?" Ruan noticed the steaming kettle, the mug set close to it, and poured hot water over instant hot chocolate, as if that would calm down the prickling tension between them—the sense that everything was moving too fast for them both.

"It's fine," Sam said again. "I'm used to it. I need to . . . uh—" he gestured at his wet boxers. The cold water hadn't left him much to work with, but Ruan eyed the shape of him under the clinging material anyway. "Take these off. Get changed."

His clothes were folded over the same wooden frame where the towel had been warming, but Ruan said, "I'll get the duvet from the van. Don't feel you need to get dressed again for my sake. I like the view."

Sam smiled, like he was a little shocked but not averse. "You're very presumptuous," he teased.

"Well, I feel like a conquering hero come to claim his reward." Ruan grinned back, and fished the MacBook out from behind his back. "I went into the lair of the beast for this, right enough. I reckon I'm at least owed a kiss."

"My laptop!" Sam dropped the towel and reached for it with both hands, joy and relief making his worn face radiant as the blaze at his back. His milk-white skin had begun to blush up calves and buttocks and over his shoulders as the warmth of the fire did its work. "How did you get it?"

"I've been sworn to secrecy on that part," Ruan said with some regret. He'd have liked to tell the story, to get the admiration that was his due, but he couldn't tell. You didn't tell outsiders anything, or you deserved what came to you. "But it's yours, is it? With that pentagram on it and all?"

Sam's uncomprehending look was desperately reassuring. "What, this?" he said, showing Ruan the picture that he'd not been able to forget all trip. "This is a tarot card—the Ace of Pentacles? It symbolizes prosperity and new starts. It's a protective sign. Also I just like the picture."

Of course a sensible person wouldn't take the potential criminal's word for it, but right now Ruan was thinking that sense was overrated.

At once, presumably checking on its well-being like an anxious parent, Sam switched his computer on. So Ruan tore himself away from gazing at him long enough to drag the duvet and another mug out of the van. When he returned, Sam had honest to God kicked off his boxers and was sitting in the firelit clearing nude, with the final pennants of fiery sunset above him and his perfect lips lit up blue as his eyes from the light of his screen.

"It's fine." He lifted his head as Ruan approached, his face softened by joy, his eyes shining. "It doesn't look like they got past the password."

"What about my kiss, then?" Ruan's face ached in response as his smile stretched his cheeks. Sam'd been told not to dress, and he hadn't dressed. That was a yes, wasn't it?

Ruan still came close gradually. No sense in rushing, no sense in spurning something so rare as this guy's trust. When he reached out at first, it was only to settle the duvet around Sam's shoulders, tug him closer by the ends of it, not yet daring to touch.

Sam's fingers strayed to the ends of Ruan's scarf. He unwound it deliberately, letting it fall to the tussocky grass. Ruan felt the warmth of the fire touch his skin, followed by the soft rush of Sam's breath under his jaw as Sam breathed hard, as if nerving himself up.

Carefully, Ruan reached out and rested his fingers in the hollows of Sam's ribs. He could feel the heartbeat, and the breath, and Sam's stubborn fight for the resolve to move forward. He didn't think he'd ever felt so powerful or so trusted as he did when Sam finally raised his head and leaned up the inch or so between them to touch those perfect pink lips to his own.

It took them all evening, wrapped in the bedclothes, kissing, occasionally breaking apart to tend the fire, before they worked up the courage to try rubbing off, gently and slowly in the warmth. Sam fell asleep afterwards, curled against Ruan's chest, the crown of his head under Ruan's chin. Ruan lay awake, watching the stars, feeling the cold begin to bite again at the planes of his face, and wondering if he'd done the right thing.

CHAPTER THIRTEEN

Sam woke to a more than physical warmth. Saturated by contentment, he tried to separate out the elements that made this awakening so much better than . . . any he could ever remember.

His feet were certainly very cold, and resting against something spiky. He drew up his knees to slide them back into the bedclothes, and his knees brushed against the lax thigh of Ruan Gwynn. One of Ruan's arms was under his cheek, curled around the top of his head and holding him close. The other draped over his ribs with a reassuring weight. For a blessed moment before he fully woke, everything in Sam's mind was silent and satisfied, and he basked in the embrace like a cat in sunlight.

Then a spatter of cold water hit his ear and the crown of his head. The final embers of the night's fire hissed as drenching December rain rolled over them, hammering into his bedding and the clothes that hung abandoned on the rack by the fire. His suddenly woken mind hissed in echo: *How could you be so stupid? Now your duvet's wet and you'll be sleeping in damp sheets for the next month. Probably get pneumonia, end up in the hospital, and then* they'll *come and get you, and you'll never have another morning of waking up with him.*

Ruan had woken at some point in this mental diatribe. He had scrambled to his feet, taking the bedding with him. Sam shivered at the blast of cold, but his internal shriek of *God, I bet he thinks you're such an idiot. I bet he's angry now. He's going to shout and storm off and you won't see him again now he's got what he wants*, was derailed by Ruan's laugh. The man wasn't fox-like at all, whatever Sam's dreams might have tried to tell him, more of a black Labrador, sleek dark hair already plastered to his head, his face turned up into the downpour in a bounding delight, laughing like this was all the best of fun.

"My laptop!" Sam exclaimed. It had been in the duvet with them, but it was probably drenched and dead. He tried to feel for it in the great swath of material in Ruan's arms, while the rain beat on his back, and Ruan fended him off with a bare arm.

"Inside!" Ruan gasped, bounding away towards the van. It wasn't locked—the door opened easily and they bundled inside and stood, catching up with themselves in the shelter while Ruan's long hair dripped on the floor, and Sam wrestled the lump in the duvet and recovered his entirely unharmed, dry computer.

With that anxiety relieved, he was free to join in with Ruan's laughter until his teeth started to clatter. "I'm—" he stuttered in the cold, "I'm sorry."

"About the rain?" Ruan grinned. "'S'not your fault." He didn't *look* disgusted or angry or even disappointed. Nothing Sam might need to fix. In fact he looked radiant, with the laugh settled down to a big beaming smile, as though everything was still perfect, as though Sam had not yet done anything wrong. Then he shuddered too. "Shit, I am cold though. Oh my god, my nuts are frozen right off."

"I'd say we should go back to bed and I'd see if I could find them," Sam chuckled, relaxing a little about the whole morning-after-the-night-before awkwardness. "But there's no warmth left in this wet bedding. I'm going to have to pay to get it tumble dried." He sighed, though not as deeply as he might have done. A tiny corner of his heart remained stubbornly bright, as though last night's golden sunset had taken up permanent residence there.

"You know what I think?" Ruan began struggling into his own clothes—they too had been inside the duvet, though the boots were currently filling with water outside. "We need a good cooked breakfast somewhere warm. Shove this bedding in a bag, put your spare clothes on, and come with me."

The trudge into town with wet shoes rubbing his feet raw and his wet clothes clinging to his skin, his bones feeling like they would never be warm again, should not have been joyful, but it was. They were the only pedestrians out in the downpour this early in the morning—the sun barely a grey streak on the horizon. The rain had closed around them like curtains, and in that dark privacy they walked shoulder to shoulder. Ruan's hand had sought his out very early on, and the clasp of their fingers felt oddly powerful when it was the only spark of warmth in the whole world.

Sam had been expecting to end up at a café. Maybe one next door to a launderette. That would have been convenient, if expensive. But Ruan led him all the way down to a street off the seafront, where the chill of the air was brutal, and the rain mixed with spume from the angry waves. There a core of positively ancient houses huddled at the cobble-lined end of the oldest part of town, and Ruan unlocked the crimson-painted door of an unsteady cottage and pushed him inside.

Sam slicked the water from his hair, watched it drip from the hems of his trousers and his coat onto red and brown tiles. A small radiator against the wall gave out something he felt as painful static for a long time before his body warmed up enough to recognise it as heat.

"Mam?" Ruan stripped off coat, hoodie, T-shirt, boots, and socks as he yelled.

"In here!" a woman shouted from further down the corridor and to the left.

"We been caught out in the rain. Can you put breakfast on for me and Sam?"

Following Ruan's hand signals, Sam had taken off his coat, but he hadn't dared to dump it in the pile of wet clothes. He drew it in towards himself like a shield as a woman with henna-red hair leaned out from the distant doorway and examined him. He swallowed, wondered if he should wave or walk forward so that he could shake her hand, or God forbid, go in for the continental hug. If he'd known they were coming to Ruan's house, he'd have been more terrified. He simply wouldn't have come. It was horrifying, knowing that she probably had a good idea what they'd been up to last night.

But then she smiled, and suddenly he could see where Ruan got his grin. "No sense at all," she said, shaking her head. "You get out of those wet things. Towels in the airing cupboard. Breakfast'll be on the table when you're done."

Ruan kissed him as he was towelling his hair a few minutes later, already warming up now he was wearing a pair of Ruan's skinny jeans—large on him—and a hand-knitted jumper of Dennis-the-Menace stripes. "It'll be fine," Ruan said, and Sam managed to believe him all the way down the stairs.

The scrubbed oak kitchen table was big enough for eight, the floor here also tiled, but covered with mismatched rugs. A brown-haired child of indeterminate sex was mopping up bean juice with a slice of toast, but scraped their chair back immediately on seeing Sam, and left the room just as Ruan's mother put down two plates of cooked breakfast and turned off the cooker to go stuff their clothes into the washing machine.

"I . . ." Sam tried, not knowing what he was trying to say, but overwhelmed by gratitude and shame. Surely he wasn't worthy of this kind of welcome?

"You look like you could do with a proper meal," she said, measuring out washing powder. "Don't worry about Jimmy now, he's shy. And the others . . ." she raised a hand, drawing his attention to the footsteps thudding on the ceiling above, the sound of opening drawers and two different blended radios, "they'll be down and out in no time. I've got to go, so you can put that through the tumble dryer yourself when it's washed, okay?"

Again, it was all so easy it made his mind go blank. "Thank you," he managed at last, and it didn't seem nearly enough, but it made her smile as she left.

This strange obliging universe into which he had fallen was going to burst at some point. It would burst and he'd be out in the cold. But that was all the more reason to hold on tight while he could.

The kitchen had both a radiator and an old iron range. As they set to eat, there was a long silence filled only with the taps, pings, and creaks of hot metal and the gurgling trundle of the washing machine. Sam chewed fried mushrooms and onions, wanted to ask, *Why are you doing this? Why have you adopted—rescued me?* But it was too pathetic to let out loud.

"What should I say to the police about the computer?" he tried instead. "If I can't tell them where you found it?"

Ruan dissected his fried egg with a faint movement of the shoulders that might have been a shrug. "I don't know. Say you didn't realize you'd left it in the car. Say it was all a misunderstanding—you never lost it at all."

"Why?" The word was out before Sam had thought it through. What if he didn't want to hear the reason? What if it was something terrible?

The little shrug again, almost sullen, and see, he *didn't* want to hear it. He didn't want to make Ruan uncomfortable.

"It's a Lusmoore thing. I promised not to tell."

Sam had no idea what that meant, but he recognized the signs of someone being forced into a place they didn't want to go. Here, with the big clock ticking and the rain against the windows, he had no desire whatsoever to push Ruan any further.

"Okay," he agreed. "I'm just glad to have it back. I don't suppose you have the computers of the other girls who are being targeted? This fat girl in 4G, for example? I'd like to cross-reference whatever comments are on her accounts, and they'll all need checking for viruses."

Ruan pushed his now-empty plate away and took Sam's hand. A little moment of shock at the contact passed into pleasant tingling and a curl of blended fondness and arousal.

"I'll ask Tegan to ask around," Ruan said, rubbing a thumb across his knuckles, tender and surprisingly intimate. "But I thought while we were here—around my bed—I could take you up on that offer you made this morning. I don't think you'd have as far to look now. I'm mostly restored."

"There are . . ." A great hot swell of nerves and excitement and terror went over Sam at the thought. "There are people in the house. I mean it's your house. And they're your people. And they're here."

His own parents had very much had a "not under my roof" policy, and a preternatural sense for anyone bending the rules enough even to kiss. He couldn't shake the conviction that it was obscene and wrong to use a bed in one's parents' house for anything other than sleeping. What if he just *couldn't*? What if he was dreadful, and Ruan was disappointed or, worse, contemptuous?

"They'll all be—" Ruan started, as a phone rang in the corridor of the hall, and a portly older man with Ruan's Roman nose burst through the kitchen door and slammed a cereal packet and a bowl onto the table.

"Will you get that?" he said to Ruan, nodding to Sam as he poured milk and shovelled in the cereal, taking the bowl with him as he strode out to shout up the stairs, "You've got ten minutes for breakfast if you still want a lift."

Ruan disappeared into the hall and returned with a cordless handset cradled against his shoulder. "Yes? Last night you say? Oh, this morning?"

Sam watched as Ruan's frown smoothed into the return of his delighted smile. Both he and Ruan's father watched intently as Ruan thumbed the phone off and raised both hands in a kind of *I said so. Didn't I say so?* gesture, calling Heaven to witness.

"Yes!" he hissed, triumphant. "I mean, I shouldn't be glad, but I knew it wasn't you. I knew it all along. That was Auntie Jennifer. She's asking if we can go up and see her. Another one of her sheep's been . . . mutilated, and it happened last night, after midnight, when you were with me."

CHAPTER FOURTEEN

While they'd been upstairs changing, some obliging person had stuffed their boots with scrunched-up newspaper and placed them upside down on top of the radiator in the hall. When Sam pulled his on, they were already almost dry, the small amount of dampness left easily fended off by his socks. Back home, he would have just had a second or third pair to pull on, and would have thought nothing of it, but over the last half year he'd learned the value of dry footwear, and the little gesture made an unexpected sob catch at the base of his throat.

He concealed it by bending over and carefully stuffing the too-long legs of his trousers into the boots and lacing them up over the top. Ruan's jumper smelled like him, and also like sheep. Heavy, slightly rough wool, warm and scratchy and rain-resistant, the lanolin still in it.

"You all right?" Ruan asked, dropping a hand on his back when he didn't straighten up once his laces were tied. Sam squinched his eyes shut, got a hold on the desire to weep, and rose.

"I'm fine. Everyone's so kind, and I . . ." *I'm not used to it* would sound too pathetic, so Sam didn't say it, but Ruan's liquid look suggested that he'd heard it anyway.

"Your family's not like this?" Ruan sounded tentative, as though he didn't quite understand how a family could work differently.

"They're not *cruel*," Sam felt obliged to say. "They would just have complained more. They'd have made you feel exactly how stupid and irresponsible you'd been to be caught out in the rain. How much work you'd made for everyone. How many hundreds of pounds damage the water had done to the carpet. 'Darling, are you incapable of behaving like an adult? Should I find you a nanny?'"

And now he was being petty, ugly, angry, and anyone in their right mind should run away. He pushed the anger to the background and let the guilt soak through him like the rain.

"Blimey," said Ruan. "Remind me not to go round there with my boots on. At least Jennifer won't mind. She's in and out all day tracking mud after her. You take that umbrella now. I'm going to be prepared this time."

That umbrella was a lady's pocket brolly with a map of the London Underground on it. Ruan took a larger striped camping umbrella with him, though they found on opening the door that the rain had eased a little. There was still an enchantment about retracing their path with a roof held over their heads, and Sam watched the jellyfish-like domes of the umbrellas and their silver tendrils of water with a sense that something bruised inside him was beginning to heal.

Ruan no longer thought that he was the sheep killer. Ruan's family didn't think it either. Sam had his laptop back and an important job to do with it. That part was scary, but it was a job he knew was within his capabilities. He was returning to Auntie Jennifer's not as a suspect but as a helper, and it was a new day. A day on which he might not screw up too much, please God.

And, unlikely though it sounded, this thing with Ruan had not ended with a one-night stand. It seemed to be continuing, and despite the ever-present bite of pain across Sam's chest, the part of him that was waiting for disaster, he hadn't ballsed it up yet.

A slight woman in stripy pyjamas met them at the farmhouse door. It was the first time Sam had seen the place in the light of day, and yes, he could see why no one here would shed a tear over a bit of water. The window-ledges were mossy and cracked, the paint on the front door faded and flaky. The farm's outer yard was an ankle-deep mud bath in which a disconsolate tractor rusted. A sheep dip and shearing shed nearby filled the early morning with a scent of chemicals and dung.

"She's up at Sir Richard." The woman moved aside as a sheepdog rocketed past her to cavort and gambol around Ruan in oddly silent joy. It stood on its hind legs to try to lick his face, the feathers of its tail whipping Sam's leg as it wagged. Ruan laughed and grabbed it by the chin, holding its face away from him while his other hand rubbed across its ears and down the length of its panting throat.

"All right, Tiger, come by," said the woman indulgently, wilting a little, putting out a hand to the doorframe as if she needed its support. She had a nice face—blunt-cut but kindly—with no colour in it, the lips as white as the cheeks. Sam hadn't been introduced, but he put two and two together and excused Jennifer some of her anger, some of her pinched expressions. He wondered if the illness was serious, if this woman was a sister or a good friend or a lover. But he didn't ask. That would have been rude.

Ruan reluctantly stopped tussling with the dog. Well trained, it went to its owner's side at once and sat there, watching Sam with alert amber eyes, its mouth half open, looking as though it were grinning. Sam smiled at it. How well turned out it was—a black dog with a shirt-front of white and just a tiny little nick of white on the tip of one ear. It beat its tail twice against the floor as if they'd reached an understanding.

"I'm going to sit down."

"You all right, Alana?" Ruan asked, starting forward as though to go inside when the woman eased herself to a bench by the side of the hall, but Alana raised a hand and shooed him off.

"It's only the flu. Don't fuss, but don't come near either. I don't want to pass it along. You go on up to Dicky. Your auntie Jennifer, she's . . . she's rattled by this one. I can tell. She'll be glad of you."

The rain blew off towards the sea as they walked uphill. Thick grey clouds thinned until ragged patches of sky opened above, and misty sunrays swept the hummocky ground, casting in high relief the tall, single standing stone they were walking towards. With the sun behind it, it was a raised middle finger to the mainland beyond.

"Dicky?" Sam asked as he tramped, relief and satisfaction and a good breakfast still making him feel like he was equal to anything.

"It's the stone's name." Ruan grinned. "Sir Richard, for long. It's supposed to be one of King Arthur's lads, turned into stone by the Black Knight. That's what we tell the tourists anyway. And 'dicky' works well enough for the people who think it's something in the fertility line."

"People think it's a phallus?" Sam looked again at the menhir now the angle had changed, and he could see its grey shape more clearly. Aside from the fact that it was tall and vaguely cylindrical, the top tapering off a little, he didn't see the resemblance himself. Just a roughly wrought stone pillar standing alone in a pinkish puddle of water. "You'd expect a sacrifice for fertility there then, not a curse. Unless . . ."

They were close enough now to see movement beyond the stone, and a black, inchoate mass, flapping and fidgeting halfway up it. Ruan stopped next to Sam and shuddered all over. That was when Sam realized that the grin had fallen from Ruan's face and that he was shaking, frightened.

"I . . ." said Ruan in a small voice. "I might just stay here. I don't like . . . I don't like any of it."

Strange to feel there was anything Sam wasn't scared of that Ruan was, but that, too, was a relief. He'd been taking a lot in this relationship. It was nice to think he could give back.

"It can't hurt you," he said, intellectually interested in Ruan's genuine fear. Sam's own agnosticism remained unruffled and unconcerned, which was surely odd considering how many other things gave him the heebie-jeebies. "Even if you believe this stuff works, it hasn't been aimed at you. Also, looking at it can't possibly be worse than the things you imagine because you didn't see."

Jennifer stepped out from behind the stone's wide girth, water dripping from her flat cap, her hands coated with brownish gore. She narrowed her eyes at Sam. "You're here again, I see."

"He didn't do this, Auntie," Ruan got in before Sam could open his mouth. "I were with him all last night, from sunset on."

"Oh you were, were you?" Jennifer took off her cap and thwacked it hard against her leg a couple of times, scattering droplets before putting it back on again dry. In the time this gave her to think, her mouth turned up at one corner. Then she gave a harrumph and turned the other corner up too. "All right, then. Come over and look if you like, Mr. 'I'm an expert in magic but I didn't have nothing to do with this.'"

Sam came, and after all his brave words, it still made the hair creep on his head. This was worse. Much worse. The sheep lay in the hollow beneath the standing stone as the last one had, cut open and eviscerated, with a pentagram above the bleeding stump of its neck. The head had been sawn off.

Above the sacrifice, a human figure had been hung from a noose of rope tied around the ancient stone. For a moment he thought it was a real person. Terror gutted his earlier serenity, and then he saw it was a scarecrow. A scarecrow dressed in good quality tweed trousers and jacket, what might have been a blue jumper before it had been drenched in streams of blood. The head of the sheep had been mounted on the scarecrow's neck and was held in place by several long scarves of black gauze, staple-gunned into the straw. That was what had given the impression of a cloud of dark movement, as the gauze had been raised and stirred by the wind.

Sharpened stakes, of the vampire-killing sort, had been driven into the scarecrow's heart and groin. The whole thing was written over with a mad scribbling of those symbols that meant nothing to Sam, crosshatching the stone and the sheep's face in lines of gleaming silver.

"Well, I think we can safely say he doesn't mean anything good by it," Sam said, in an attempt to lighten the mood.

"No shit, Sherlock." Jennifer laughed, but there was an edge in it, as though she was only just holding herself back from screaming. She shook her head. "I don't know who this bastard is, or what he thinks I've done to him. If he'd come to me with his grievance, I'd've put it right. But this? How am I supposed to mend this when he won't even say who he is or what I've done?"

"I thought you didn't believe in this stuff?" Sam tried, at a loss. Admittedly, this was nastier than the last, but he wasn't yet seeing why Jennifer was so much more upset by it.

"I don't know if I do." Jennifer threw her hands up and wheeled to face the sea. Everything was silver out there—the waves, the moving rays of sunshine, the pearly sky. "I don't know if I do, all right? But I do believe whoever did this is out to get me. I'll tell you something for free, shall I? Those clothes? They came out of my laundry room. Sometime this week, while Alana was lying in bed ill and helpless upstairs, that bastard's been in my house and stolen my clothes. I can't stop thinking about what else he might have done instead."

CHAPTER FIFTEEN

"Y ou've told the police?" Sam's breath caught in the centre of his chest as though a ball of hooks was buried under his breastbone. He didn't really want to see the police again, but it was inevitable and would have to be endured. At least he had Ruan with him now, with an alibi.

"Oh yes." Jennifer sounded disgusted. "Pete's looking into a burglary in the Lanes, and the man I spoke to was an incomer. Not impressed by a couple of dead sheep. He said any evidence'd be washed away by the rain, and us mopping the laundry as regular, but someone'll be up today to take pictures and statements, so I'm to leave her as she lies. Bloody useless, the lot of them."

Ruan's wide, generous mouth was like a slash in his face as he chewed his lips. "Well," he said, dropping his gaze to Sam's shoes, as though he was half-ashamed to offer this idea, didn't want to be mocked for it. "What if we fight magic with magic?" And now he caught Sam's gaze, his eyes quicksilver as the rain, full of shades of trust and desperation and hope that simultaneously made Sam feel horribly responsible and almost up to the challenge. "You said you were interested in all of this, didn't you? Maybe there's some good magic that can be done to protect Jennifer and Alana and the house and the sheep? What do you think?"

The rain had fully stopped now, and a bitterly cold north wind blew Sam's fragile umbrella inside out. He struggled to put it down and gather all the frail wires of it together so it would not be damaged, rolled it up carefully, and put it in one of the deep pockets of his raincoat.

Hadn't he just been thinking how good it was to be able to give something back to Ruan? Here was another chance. But. Oh God, they kept asking things of him. Hard things with real consequences. He couldn't—

The shrill voice yammered on its own, shaking the cage of his ribs and squeezing his heart like a mad, malicious poltergeist. He was so fucking fed up of that voice. So fed up of it.

"I . . ." The echo of its silent screaming made his voice thin, reluctant, but he forced it out anyway. "I'm not . . . I mean I look things up on the internet, but I don't have any special . . . It's all theoretical, you know?"

But Jennifer had stepped closer to him now, and the hope in her face brought out a faint resemblance to Ruan—the almond shape of her eyes, perhaps, or the line of her jaw. "I like the idea of there being *something* I can do back at him. Even if it's more of this mumbo-jumbo. But let's not stand here in the cold. You have a think while we walk back to the house."

The kitchen of Jennifer's farmhouse had begun to feel familiar to Sam now. There was a comfort in the grandfather clock and the warm range, the heavy, dark dresser with its set of red-and-gold-painted plates and its collection of dusty tankards, boxes of shotgun pellets, and WD-40.

Tiger lay beneath the round table, gnawing on a bone so large Sam would have believed it belonged to a dinosaur. Alana had left a note by the kettle, *Gone back to bed*, that Jennifer crumpled and stuffed in her pocket when she saw Sam looking.

Silence fell as the water in the kettle sighed and then raged itself hot. Jennifer ladled loose tea into a pot and stamped off to open a door to an old-fashioned pantry, lined with shelves of jars and preserves. "I don't have biscuits," she said, sliding a platter containing a very large pork pie onto the table.

Tiger abandoned his bone and came to sit with his chin on Ruan's lap, gazing at him adoringly. The dark hair fell curling around Ruan's cheek, exposing once again the diamond stud in his ear, pale as a water drop now the sun wasn't on it. His beauty struck Sam all at once with an exaltation like that of music. Something almost Venetian about him in this pose. He could see da Vinci sitting where he sat, sketching Ruan in sure strokes of charcoal chiaroscuro.

Now he wasn't being accused of anything, this room felt like a sanctuary too. The quiet of it was peace, acceptance, and Sam took a mug of tea and curled his hands round it feeling soothed.

Did it matter if he didn't have any innate power or mana in him to work with? Mystic influences aside, what was being waged here was a campaign of psychological warfare. Why would it not help to provide some arms and armour to the defenders? If Jennifer thought she was being threatened, that in itself was a threat. If she thought she was being protected, wouldn't that be a protection in itself?

Sam brought his phone out. Took a sip of scalding-hot tea, red as a brick with tannin, and paged through his bookmarks of protective sigils.

The trouble was that if you *did* believe in this stuff, many of these signs were sacred to different gods, and drew their power from entities who might not like their names being taken in vain. The Helm of Odin, for example—it was aesthetically pleasing, would look good as a plaque on the house eves or as a tattoo—but inadvertently attracting the attention of the Lord of the Gallows when one wasn't prepared for it might end up being worse than the situation they were currently in. There were things you probably shouldn't be casual about, and potentially angry, immensely powerful supernatural beings was high on that list.

Already the task seemed impossible again. Impossibly dangerous. Terrifyingly easy to get wrong. He closed his eyes, aware that he was catastrophizing, but gripped rigid with the thought of failure and annihilation around every corner.

A wet, cold press on his inner wrist startled him back to life. He took a sharp breath and looked down. Tiger was at his feet now, nosing at him as if to say, *Enough of gods. Pet me.* So he did.

"I'm going to need some guidance," he admitted. "I'll run up to the van and get my tarot, if that's okay."

"I don't normally hold with it." Jennifer cut a slice of the pie and took down one of the good plates to serve it on, putting it in front of Sam as if she didn't expect him to recognize what he'd been given. Trust. Dignity. "I don't normally hold with any of this. I'm C of E. But I talked to the vicar after the first one, and he said, 'Ignore it,' so I don't see as I have much choice."

The walk did Sam good. For whatever brief period, the sun was out, making it easier to relax about the responsibilities he was intent on shouldering. It surprised Sam to find his van less appealing than the cosy warmth of Jennifer's kitchen, but he didn't give it much thought as he pocketed his cards and went back.

"Okay." He shuffled the pack beneath the table. Jennifer had added a pot of mustard to the clutter on the table, and its faintly acrid smell mixed with the tea and the burning wood from the stove to create a scent that tingled as he breathed. "I'm just going to do a basic three cards layout. This," he drew the first and laid it facedown in front of him, slightly to the left, "is the past, what has brought us to this point. A summary of what we're facing. This next one," in the middle, "represents what options are available to us in the present. And this last one," to the right, "shows us what kind of results are going to come. Clear?"

Jennifer shrugged from where she was crouched by the fuel door of the stove, adding more wood. "I guess." But Ruan got up and came around the table to lean over Sam's shoulder, one hand on the edge of the table and the other on his neck.

"Okay. Let's look at what we're up against." Sam turned the card over. Goat's head and horns, lolling tongue, and the world in flames beneath. The hand on his neck clenched suddenly, hard enough to bruise, as Ruan recoiled.

"The devil?" he squeaked. "It's the actual devil doing this?"

In another context, Sam might have found that funny, but he didn't like to see Ruan scared. "It's okay, it's fine," he insisted. "In fact it's quite good. This is a card about materialism. Um, greed, possessiveness. This is basically the card I associate with my family. Which . . . no. This is not their style. If they wanted to scare someone, they'd do it with a lawsuit. But no, this doesn't represent the actual devil."

Strange. He would have automatically assumed that witchcraft was a spiritual rather than a material threat. It made him think again of the nonsensical symbols and wonder if they'd ever meant anything at all, or if they'd just been made up for effect. "I don't see how this can be about money, though. Pride or cruelty would fit better. I don't know."

"What can we do about it, then?" Ruan seemed to realize he was squeezing too hard. He brushed his thumb apologetically across Sam's throat, making him shiver, and then let go.

Sam flipped the middle card; the Sun. He frowned at its serene smiling face and stylized rays. "Well. It's a good card. It's happiness, contentment, peace of mind. Energy. But I'd rather have seen it in the results position. It doesn't really tell you what to do beyond accept that life is great. Which it's not."

He thought about the sunlight on the walk to and from his van, and how much it had made him feel better. Maybe he should take the card literally. If he was facing a materialist—not a real witch, but someone who was making things up as he went along—and *he* didn't want to get entities involved either, was there any reason why Sam shouldn't make things up too?

A wide bracelet of red and black ink circled Ruan's left wrist, poking out from his sleeve as he rested that hand against the table. Sam looked at it, and everything came together into an idea that made him laugh with surprise. "Oh!" Wouldn't it be good if he could take the peace of mind that the sun gave and actually insert it directly into Jennifer's body? Light, power, happiness, under the skin. Surely that would help. "Oh, okay. I've got an idea."

"What is it?"

"Let me check the results card first."

He flipped the last card and sighed with satisfaction. "Ah, yes. See—this is Justice. Wrongs righted, turbulent emotions balanced at last. It's going to work." It was so much easier to breathe and to think when the cards were taking responsibility for him. If terror came, if these choices proved to be the wrong ones, at least he'd have the comfort that it wasn't entirely his fault.

"This is what I want you to do, to protect you from the malice of your attacker. I want you or Jennifer to take a vial of your tattoo ink and keep it in direct sunlight all day long, so that the power of the sun can infuse it. Then I want you to use that ink to tattoo this symbol," he drew a quick sketch of the elder Futhork Sowilo rune inside a simple rayed sun, "over your heart chakra. That's here." He demonstrated with a thumb on his own chest. "I mean, over Jennifer's. And Alana's too, just to be sure."

It was Jennifer's turn to come close, peering at the symbol with a sceptical eye. "And that'll do the trick, will it? Protect us from this bastard?"

Sam wasn't sure that the symbol would protect them by itself, but he was certain that having something they believed was protecting them literally encoded into their bodies would be strengthening. The belief that it would help would be a help in itself, and the commitment involved in a tattoo would make them take it more seriously, and would last a lifetime. What better way to give oneself permanent confidence than to insert it directly beneath one's skin? "It won't protect you per se," he clarified. "But it will give you the energy, the peace of mind, the clarity, and the *power* you need to protect yourself."

Silence again, and then Jennifer shrugged. "I don't see it'll do any harm, at least. I'll try it." But for all her nonchalance, it was the first time her face had relaxed enough for her laugh lines to be more prominent than her frown.

Ruan leaned down to kiss Sam's neck where his hand had been. "Thank you."

And Sam found himself glowing. He'd achieved something. He'd actually helped. Who would have thought it?

I can do other things, he thought, in the flush of bravery that followed. *Practical things. I'm not going to stop at mumbo-jumbo. I'm going to solve this for him.* In the light of Ruan's belief in him, he could almost bring himself to believe it too.

CHAPTER SIXTEEN

Techno-wizard, see. He'd been right the first time.

Ruan held that close for the rest of the day. They'd already lost the morning's light, and the police came soon after for yet more statements and photos, so it wasn't as though he could start straightaway. The delay gave him a chance to really appreciate Sam Atkins proper, now he knew the man hadn't done anything wrong.

Watching him with his computer and his cards, interrogating the mysteries of the universe, past and future, the same way he'd query an IP address—there was something very satisfying about that. He looked the part, with that twelve-carat-gold hair and that ethereal slenderness. Like an angel that hadn't fallen so much as come out for a day trip to Earth and got lost.

To be absolutely certain of getting the first light tomorrow, he didn't go back with Sam to his van, just sent him off with a kiss and his freshly laundered duvet and set his own alarm for six in the morning. It turned out to be a long night in a bed that shouldn't have felt cold or empty—for God's sake, he'd only ever slept with Sam once, he couldn't be addicted already—but did. He only got to sleep by 2 a.m., and then his dreams were full of blood and darkness, of devils, and of Sam with the sun in his hair, driving them off. He woke to a vivid memory of Sam shuddering in his arms, the surprising strength in those skinny limbs, the warmth and zeal of his surrender. It felt almost blasphemous for a moment after he'd finished off alone.

Six in the morning and four hours' sleep. Rolling out of bed with a headache that he treated with coffee and painkillers, he packed himself sandwiches, crisps, and a thermos of tea and considered his options on ink.

He'd assumed black at first, but why not yellow, like the sun's face, or the sheen of Sam's hair? Why not white, as a symbol for goodness? Something about a white protective tattoo appealed to him. It'd look like a scar, and it would be secret—something you'd know was there but wouldn't have to be obvious about.

But maybe secrecy was their opponent's way. Maybe being out there and in your face about it—honest as the day is long—was more appropriate for good magic?

He brushed his tangled curls and shrugged into the warmest coat he had, and two pairs of insulated socks. That thing on Jennifer's land had knocked the heart right out of him, but thinking about Sam's protective charm was putting it back, and extra. Because this was awesome. This might be the angle he needed to make a go of the tattoo business.

Magic tattoos! Maybe if there were different potions or the like, he could mix them in the shading water. Red tattoos for bravery, blue for . . . There, his knowledge ran out. He'd have to ask Sam. He'd have to get Sam involved in it somehow, figuring out what sigils to choose, where they should go. People would want that, wouldn't they? He certainly would. The idea was making his head fizz with plans.

Pulling his stash of inks out from under his bed, he took a vial of black, one of white, and one of yellow, wrapped them tenderly in a handkerchief, and put them in his pocket. Then cramming on his hat and scarf, he set off at a fast pace for St. Ia's.

The vicar might not have believed in exorcism or the literal fight against the dark arts, but he kept the church unlocked. Ruan fumbled through the dark porch and eased open the heavy oak door, stepping into faint warmth. After the walk in the dark, the candles by the sacristy safe, on the altar, and in front of the rough statue of St. Ia threw gold bubbles of light in the brown velvet dimness. Enough so, he could walk up the stairs to the balcony that encircled the whole room, and take up position in the eastern window to greet the dawn.

He nodded in the silence. He'd not been asked to come here, but it had seemed right. Jennifer would be happier, certain sure, to know that God had been involved in this somewhere, and Ruan could move from window to window around the whole clerestory to follow the sun without having to stay outside all day long. It might rain, after all. And he could get a good phone signal in St. Ia's, ironically enough, given that they asked you to turn it off at the door.

He unwrapped his inks and placed them in the window to catch the dawn. By now it was half seven and other people would be getting up, getting ready for school. Time to do something on the other problem, then. He gave it another half an hour, watching the sky turn pale out of the window, and then phoned Tegan to remind her that Sam needed the other girls' help if he was ever to track their bully down.

"I've told 'em already," she said, sounding grumpy and barely awake. "Everyone's bringing their laptops in even if they wouldn't have normally. We'll come up to that bloke's van after school today with them, and he can doctor them then."

"Can you make it later?" Ruan imagined the kind of meltdown that might be inspired by a hoard of schoolchildren descending on Sam unannounced. "I can't come until after the sun sets, and that's about four-ish. You arrive at five, I can be there."

"You a vampire now, Uncle Ruan?" She snorted.

"Don't!" In the light of all the witchcraft going around, he was not as amused as he might have been. "I'll tell you about it when you get there. Five all right?"

"Yeah, we'll go for chips first. See ya!"

He phoned Sam next and explained the plan, half hoping that Sam would offer to come to the church and keep him company.

But Sam said, "Oh. Do you know how many there'll be?" and when Ruan said he didn't, but maybe quite a few, he said, "I'd better get ready," as though he had a mansion to spring clean, and rang off.

"Wow, Mr. Atkins, this is so cool!"

The teens had turned up en masse at twenty past five and were looking around the clearing with wide eyes. Ruan had to agree with them. Sam had been hard at work. Now the fire burnt brightly, ringed with grey stones. The fallen wood—rotting beneath the trees, catching on clothes, sprouting mushrooms and making the paths inaccessible—had been gathered and cut up, stacked in a lattice pattern beneath a tarpaulin to dry.

The windbreak had been extended to ring the fire on all sides, and within this ring Sam had built a sort of canvas igloo. Newly cut branches had been bent into semicircular arches, held down with rope and hand-cut pegs, with more canvas tied over the top and then buried in ferns and bracken and dried dead leaves, held on with a thin mesh net.

The tree which had fallen last autumn, blocking the way out, had been cut into sections and the sections rolled around the fire to serve as benches. The final one stood upright like an anvil, with an axe and a bow saw propped against it.

A small generator thrummed to itself beneath the van, barely having to work at all to power the lantern that swung from the nearest tree.

"It's my summer setup." Sam actually blushed, making a touching picture with his greened, scraped arms and blistered hands. "I made sure I had what I needed before I started with this life."

Ruan sank onto one of the benches and watched the girls examine the bender tent and prod at the fire. Sarah, the "fat girl"—who was in his opinion only barely plump—smiled for the first time on being shown how to hook the kettle on its springy stand over the fire, and all of the girls beamed like little kids for a moment as they took in the scene.

"I wondered what you'd have to do all day," Ruan replied, "but now I'm thinking I underestimated you. I don't know why you think you're fragile. Look at this! You're fucking Bear Grylls."

Sam laughed, clearly bashful. "I went on a course. It's not hard. It's all mechanical, conceptually simple. Not like people. Can you get them to give me their laptops? I should get started."

"Next time we come up here we're bringing marshmallows!" Tegan exclaimed, sprawling out on the raised platform bed inside the igloo. "Are we going to tell ghost stories while he does his computer whispering bit? Cos, like, with the fire and the mutilated sheep nearby it'd be—"

"No." Ruan grabbed the closest laptop back defensively. "No, we are not talking about ghosts or magic or anything like that right now. You show some respect to your auntie Jennifer. That stuff's not for fun."

He took the laptop—Kasey Sutherland's, apparently—to the camping table where Sam was arranging the others. Despite having gone to the trouble of organizing his clearing to welcome visitors, Sam was doing his best not to have to speak to anybody, and it seemed the girls knew what that was like. They had handed over their machines and then gone to sit by the fire.

Already, Sam was hunched over in total absorption, only turning his head slightly to move from one screen to the next, his tired face blue-lit by the screens, filling up his sheets of paper with crabbed illegible notes.

Ruan recognized the look of a man concentrating hard on his art, and left him to it, going to sit by the fire with the girls. He had an art of his own to practice. On coming out of the church, he'd decided he couldn't wait before trying out the infused ink, so he'd swung past home and brought his gun, a pocket full of packets of sterile needles and alcohol wipes, a battery and transformer to power it with, and a roll of cling film.

The girls had been talking movies when he started, taking off his boot and rolling down his sock to put the little symbol on the side of his calf in white ink. Not over the heart chakra, but he couldn't manage that, working one-handed on himself. It barely took ten minutes, but it felt good, clean and hot and heartening. And it wasn't in the right place and it hadn't been designed for him, but the sting of it still took away some of the memory of sheep skull and gore and malice.

He wrapped it, and when he looked up found himself the centre of a circle of fascinated eyes.

Oh. Things clicked. If ever there were people who would also benefit from permanent protection, permanent courage, it was these girls.

"What's that?" Maryam asked, peering at the design now partially concealed beneath the plastic wrap.

"It's kind of a magic tattoo." Ruan floated the idea nervously. "For protection against evil. Sam's idea—the ink's got the sun in it, and the symbol's a sun disc, so you'll always have the light right under your skin, ready to call on if you need it."

"I want one."

They'd all drawn close. Now Maryam stepped into his space, almost touching him. The hunger on all their faces was a more extreme reaction than he'd hoped for or wanted. Were Muslims allowed to get tattoos? He didn't know.

"I can't give them to anyone that's not eighteen. Not without your parents' permission. I'm sorry. That's the law."

"I'm eighteen." Kasey hunted in her pocket and brought out an ID that she pushed under Ruan's nose with an insistence that he might have read as arrogant but he now suspected was actually just desperate. "You can do me."

He could. And if it would help, why shouldn't he? "White ink like this?" he asked. "Somewhere where it's not on show all the time?"

"You got other colours that'll do the same thing?" she asked, aggression easing as she guessed he was going to agree. The ring of other girls tightened in closer, reminding him of those Victorian operation spectators where everyone was trying to stare right into the wound.

"I got red and black, but—"

"I want it here, on the back of my hand, black as it'll go," she insisted. "I want to be always seeing it."

She was a tall, awkward girl with lank black hair and bad acne, a very flat chest, a masculine jaw, and an Adam's apple. Ruan thought of his brother Jimmy and came to the painful conclusion that he would give her absolutely anything she asked for.

"You sure you want people to see it, right off? What about job interviews and such?" he asked, just in case she was thinking of a career where a tattoo would matter.

But she laughed, "I'm going on my dad's trawler, aren't I? He don't mind."

"All right." Ruan angled himself better on the bench, took out his water-based marker and nodded. "Come and sit down here and tell me how large you want it."

She was smiling by the time he wrapped her hand and went through the aftercare instructions. A soft, radiant smile. Maybe just from the endorphin buzz, or maybe because she finally felt she had something on her side, bringing her hope.

"It works," she said, holding out her hand before her as if she could see the light inside it. "It really does work. I can feel it."

"I'm glad for you," Maryam managed, sounding creditably genuine about it. "But that doesn't help the rest of us."

"I know what will, though," Sam broke in, rising from his circle of electronics like the lady from the lake. "This bastard who's been harassing you all? He made two mistakes. One on Maryam's Tumblr, one actually in the code of a virus on Sarah's." He grinned a slow, triumphant grin. "I think I've got him."

CHAPTER SEVENTEEN

Sam's grin of triumph didn't survive the impact of Ruan's excited whoop and air-punch. The reaction that had been meant to let him know how proud of him Ruan was, how impressed, only made him flinch and turn his face away. "But I don't think you're going to like it."

It wasn't one of the girls themselves was it? That was Ruan's first thought, looking at Sam's unhappy face. How terrible it would be if one of the girls had betrayed the others. Then a worse suspicion—it might be someone in Ruan's family. That slapped him in the face like a vat of acid, but he rejected it as impossible instantly, and then was ashamed that he'd ever had it at all.

"I want to know anyway," he insisted. But the pause had sobered him enough to realize that this was only the first step. Now there was the police to be involved or the bastard to be handled in some other way. There'd be painful confrontations and confessions, a long road to go before the girls got peace, even if they had finally, *finally* found their culprit. "The girls deserve to know."

Sam cast him an appealing look as though he was asking for something but he couldn't say it while he was in company. Which was sad because Ruan couldn't guess from silence and wide blue eyes. "Are you sure?"

"Yeah, I'm sure. Tell us."

"It's just that you weren't very happy last time."

Oh. Ruan remembered the empty field, the darkness under the grass—getting it now. *Oh shit.* But it was too late to back out now. He ducked his head and made a loose *whatever* gesture with both hands.

"I've . . ." Sam's voice had gone thin, breathy. The knuckles of his fingers were white where they clamped around the opposite elbow. He must be bruising himself with the intensity of his own hug. "I've traced the IP address of the originating device, and it's coming from within five hundred yards of where it told me my stolen laptop was."

His voice sped up, the pitch rising with the speed. "Um. I would like to point out that it's not my IP address and these messages both precede and antedate the time when my laptop was in that location. I don't want you to think that—"

Ruan could literally hear Sam's mind gearing up to go into a spin cycle. He was worried about himself, that was true, but he put it aside fast to step in closer to Sam and get a reassuring grip on his biceps. God, they were clamped so tight they were trembling. Sam's whole body was trembling; Ruan could feel it now he was touching, a shake like Sam was ready to die of cold.

"I don't think it was you," he said firmly. "It's okay. None of us think that. We know you wouldn't have helped us find it if you knew it was you doing it all along."

Sam blinked and took in a long shaking breath. "I suppose that's right," he said, as if it had never occurred to him that he might not be unjustly accused, that he might not find himself drummed out of town or worse. "But I don't know. I feel guilty anyway. By association."

"Whose IP is it though, Mr. Atkins?" Tegan resumed her role as spokeswoman for the girls. "That's what we want to know."

Sam collapsed back into his camping chair with a defeated expression. "I'm sorry, Tegan, and all of you. As far as I know, the map reference is in the middle of a field. I don't know what to tell you."

Again, the mute appeal to Ruan, and this time Ruan had enough context to brace himself and tell the girls. "I have an idea, but it's . . . it's Lusmoore business. I don't want you getting mixed up in it. All right?"

Tegan sneered and stepped back as if she'd been pushed.

"We are all already involved, Ruan Gwynn." Maryam reached out to take Kasey's hand, either to comfort her or to feel, through the width of her palm, the hidden sunlight of her new tattoo. "You said yourself we have the right to know."

"What are you?" Sam was hugging himself still, his trembling so bad it was now visible. "What are you involved in, Ruan? What is—"

Maybe it was the sense of responsibility or the memory of that long journey under the heavy press of the earth and the dark, when Ruan knew he was helpless? Maybe he hadn't realized quite how much that ordeal had scared him shitless, and maybe that was why he didn't wait to hear any more before he lit up with such fury they'd be able to see him from space.

"'*Involved in*'? What are you saying, Sam? You think I'd be involved in this? You think that's the kind of person I am, do you?" After all the consideration he'd shown for Sam's feelings? After he'd been on Sam's side right from the very start, even when all the evidence was against him? This was what he got, was it?

"No," Sam squeaked, barely audibly, barely getting his voice out of his throat now. Those rose-petal-pink lips that Ruan still had to watch, angry or not, were almost as white as his eyes. "Ruan, that's not—" He gasped and bent over as though his throat had closed.

Not what? Ruan waited for an explanation, already half ashamed of himself, willing, wishing to be calmed down, but Sam wasn't talking, just tilted in an awkward angle away from Ruan, taking desperate sips of air through clenched teeth.

"Not what?" Ruan insisted, the silence winding him up again. He deserved an explanation for that remark, didn't he? Sam could damn well make enough effort for that.

"I ca— I can't do this," Sam forced out, his teeth clattering. He got himself half to his feet, bent over his stomach the way he'd done the day they had first met, when he ended up with his face pressed to a tree. He staggered for his van, eyes half closed, hand outstretched for the handle. "I want you to go."

Well that was fine for him, wasn't it? He got to accuse Ruan of God knew what, though all Ruan had ever done was to try to help him. And then he got to tell Ruan when to come and when to go too? "No. I want you to tell me what you meant by that!"

Sam opened the van door, bundled himself through, and shut it. A click said it was locked, and that, too, made Ruan want to stride up and bang on the shut doors like a drum, just because he could. He took a step forward, already arguing with himself, because that would be a low thing to do to a man in the middle of an anxiety attack, especially if that was a man he . . . *cared about*. Cared about seriously, to be fair.

To his dawning gratitude, Tegan got in his way. She was as much a carrier of the famous Gwynn temper as he was, and not afraid to shout in his face if she thought the occasion deserved it. "You're being an idiot, Uncle Ruan. Go home." She cast the eye of a leader over the other girls, marshalling her troops. "We'll all go home. We'll talk about this again in the morning. To you first, and then to our dads if we need to."

The party broke up sullenly, the girls all leaving together, huddled and whispering. Ruan stood watching the shut doors of the van in the cold. Then he slunk away, the new tattoo burning as it brushed against his trouser leg all the while. By the time he got home, he was ready to head straight back.

Someone—probably his mam—had twisted a string of Christmas lights around the tree in the front garden, and when he came in, the house was decorated, multicoloured tinsel around every picture, a candlestick in the living room window, and fake snow in the corners of the upstairs bedrooms. The kitchen smelled of the first batch of mince pies, all butter and pastry, sultanas and spices. He hung up his rainbow scarf with a heavy heart and a feeling that he had no place at all in this season of goodwill.

Hiding out, he shut himself in his room, put Nine Inch Nails on in the background, and reached for his phone. The tunnels under the headland seemed to have opened up in his heart. He couldn't reach the anger anymore past the anguish of them.

Maybe the gnawing was just hunger though? Making a recce for the kitchen, he took a still-warm mince pie out of the rack and made a cup of tea, fortunate enough to get back to his room without having met anyone. Food and drink, even freshly baked, tasted like chewing cardboard and did nothing to fill the hollows inside. The prospect of trying to sleep around them was miserable. So he should do something about them, right? Right then.

Sam's voice on the other end of the phone was more welcome than any sugar hit, though it was still slurred and shaky. "Hello?"

"Sam," Ruan said, and then he couldn't go on because unexpectedly his own throat had filled up with tears.

"I'm sorry," Sam got in before him, breathless and thin sounding, as though he'd been on the rack since Ruan left. "I didn't mean that—"

Ruan's voice came loose, finally. "No, *I'm* sorry. I shouldn't have gone off like that on you. I was just . . . Are you all right?"

Sam laughed, small and indistinct over the line, like he was on the cusp of weeping too. "I'm fine. I just need you to know that I didn't . . . I didn't think you would do something like that to Maryam or anyone else. I didn't think that."

Oh. Oh no. Now Ruan felt stupid as well as guilty. "But you *said*—" he tried, not wanting to start the argument up again, but needing to understand.

"I . . . I meant that you were so secretive about the caves, last time. I wanted to know what that involved. What *is* 'a Lusmoore thing'? Are you in trouble? Can I help?"

He'd been asking what he could do to help? Ruan threw himself backward onto his bed. *You are a fucking moron, Ruan Gwynn.* But Sam was sounding stronger already, and a wave of painful relief was washing out Ruan's memory of misery. Even his guilt.

"The Lusmoores are like the local Mafia," he confessed. "They've got warehouses down in the caves under those fields. They let me in and out to get your computer, but I panicked a bit at the thought of having to go back and find out which one of 'em's sending those messages. I'm fucking scared of them, and that's no lie, but I didn't ought to have gone off on you about it."

A pause on the end of the line, and then, "So you're not breaking up with me?"

Ruan hitched himself onto his elbow and said, "No! No, never." It surprised him when he heard it, but he didn't disagree.

"And you're not angry with me anymore?" The directness of that one made him smile—simple and childish and easy to answer.

"No, no, I'm not."

"Okay." Sam sighed. When he spoke again, it was with a more determined tone. "These Lusmoores, are they after you? What can I do to make sure you're all right?"

That almost made him laugh. What—like Sam was going to stand outside the house with a shotgun to protect him rather than the other way around? The fact that it didn't seem likely didn't make it any the less charming.

"I don't think they know we're on to them yet. I'm fine. Don't worry." Ruan drew the curtain enough to check the weather. If it had been clear, he would have returned to the van. But wet snow was hissing down like white snakes, and he couldn't face another drenching. "Can I come and see you again tomorrow?"

"Please." He could tell from the tone that Sam was smiling now. A good omen for the end of the day. "Please do. We can work out some kind of plan from there."

Ruan switched the phone off a few minutes later, at peace. They had time still to think about this. There might be—there must be—a way to identify this one poisonous Lusmoore without stirring up the rest of the hive. He fell asleep certain that if anyone could do it, it would be Sam.

In the morning, he put a half dozen of the mince pies into a box and stepped out of the front door briskly, hoping for the best. It had grown even colder, and at some point in the night, the sleet must have turned into snow, because a two-inch layer of fluffy white crunched beneath his boot. He was already looking up the road towards Jennifer's farm while his hand was groping for the latch to shut the door. That was why the first thing he noticed was his fingertips sinking into a spongelike mass of cold, viscous liquid.

"Argh!" He jumped away and spun to face the object he had touched, in a twist like a cat, all the fibres in his arm shrinking as if he'd scalded them, and his heart choking the back of his throat as it swelled fit to burst.

A parcel of blood-damp cloth hung from the door handle. Two long hair-pins skewered the centre of it, scratching the door as it swayed. Though the temperature must be below freezing, the blood in which it was drenched was still wet and red. Real blood—the meat-like stink of it clear on the crisp air. If it hadn't had time either to coagulate or to freeze, the bundle must have been hung there recently. Sometime this morning, certainly. Maybe moments ago.

High on fear and anger and disbelief, Ruan pounded up the garden path, flung open the gate and looked both ways. To his right, the sea slunk sullenly at the low point of its tide. To his left an early commuter bus was pulling away from its stop. Its doors were closing, but he could see through the window well enough as the passenger sat down. A hard-faced man in his prime, with the muscles and tattoos and the flat, unblinking eyes of a Lusmoore enforcer.

CHAPTER EIGHTEEN

Shit. Shit! Ruan stepped up to the door to open it, to dive back inside, instinctively going for safety, for home. But that confronted him again with the bloody package hanging on the door. He'd touched it! He'd touched it, and if he meant to use the door handle, he would have to touch it again.

His hand stopped in the air as if repelled, even while his damp fingertips tried to chew themselves off from the inside. Now he had time to look at it, the bundle resolved itself into a rectangle of cloth wrapped around a centre that gave with a *squash*, tied with barbed wire and impaled twice with those pins. He couldn't take that thing inside his house, not inside his kitchen where Mam and Jimmy and Dad and Lora'd be eating their breakfast. Whatever it had in it, he wasn't going to bring it near them.

Backing away from it, he kept the tainted hand outstretched in front of him, like he could claim it was nothing to do with him. It still felt like ticks were crawling straight up his arm. He dropped the plastic bag with his Tupperware box of mince pies onto the snow and let himself fall into a bent-kneed crouch so he could put his left hand, his clean hand, around the still-swollen sun disc on his calf and feel the warmth of it.

It *was*—it was like curling his fingers around a lightbulb. Warmth and the sense of radiance in his palm, and he choked out a laugh because that was helping. *Sam*, he thought, gratefully. *Sam'd know what to do*, and Sam wouldn't be scared by this thing that wasn't actually worse than the other two, except for being closer to home.

Fortified, he took a few long breaths and then removed the mince pies from his carrier bag. Wrapping the bag around his hand first, he sidled up to the bundle again. Blowing his fear out on a long plume of steam, he gathered the bundle in his plastic-covered palm and drew the rest of the bag up around it, like a dog owner scooping up a turd.

Afterwards, he buried his fingertips in a drift of pristine snow, drawing them through and through it again until they were washed clean and stinging with cold. Then he touched them to the cling film that bandaged his new tattoo, as if to disinfect them. Only then did he feel human again as he stood, box of pies in one hand and curse in the other.

It seemed to glare at him all the way up to Foxglove Copse—the deathless heart of an evil genie in a Tesco carrier bag. But, as he walked, the clouds parted, and the silver-gilt winter sun came out again, first in spots and streaks sweeping over the frosted rooftops and the sleeping gardens, but then in a long great dazzle that turned the land as silver as the distant sea.

He'd already begun to feel ashamed of his terror, even before he swung over the stile onto Jennifer's land, where the sheep were the colour of stained teeth against their pristine background. Then he remembered that the tattoo had been supposed to be for Jennifer and Alana and that he'd left both gun and ink at home. What an idiot! Well, he'd have to go back for it later. He was certainly getting his exercise with all of this traipsing up and down, and it was harder to be gripped by paralysing dread in a landscape ablaze with icy light than it had been under the shadow of his porch.

As he saw the trees of Sam's copse, with all their branches aglitter from the foamy snow, and his campfire's smoke going up into the sunlight in a blue-grey pillar, he was gripped once again with awe. Villagers used to hamstring blacksmiths, didn't they? So these men that could do magic with iron couldn't run out on them, had to stay forever. They used to blind poets likewise, so he'd heard. Because when you had someone that was holy and knowledgeable and wise in things that ordinary men couldn't comprehend, you wanted to keep them, right?

Maybe that was why Sam's family had given him the crippling anxiety? Because they knew they had something magic there, in him, and they wanted to keep it. Ruan was proud of him that Sam had managed to get out anyway. He would do nothing like that. He'd make it so Sam wanted to stay, off his own bat, his own choice . . .

With that thought, enough of his un-cursed mind came back to remember what a bastard he'd been last night. The very first thing he should do when they met should be to apologize again.

Sam was stirring porridge over the fire when Ruan stepped into the clearing. He had abandoned his long raincoat and broad-brimmed hat in favour of a bulky sheepskin coat and a sheepskin hat, and might have been Kristoff from *Frozen*, if Kristoff had starved for a month beforehand.

Sam smiled on seeing Ruan, but the smile seemed wary and a little shy. Immediately Ruan felt like a douche.

"I'm sorry," he started, coming around the fire, where the warmth had melted any fallen snow and the grass still stood up green. He came to a halt close enough to gaze down on the whorl of hair on the very crown of Sam's head, a whirlpool of gold, while Sam looked up at him from the corner of a nervous blue eye. "I'm sorry I was such a bastard last night. I should have backed off when I saw you getting upset—"

"You can't not be angry when you're angry." Unexpectedly, Sam dropped the spoon in the pan and turned to hug Ruan around the thighs, cheek pressed to his hip as he had pressed it to the tree, as if to anchor himself against something solid, something reliable.

It was so sweet Ruan almost didn't think of the other possibilities, but his body was alert to them, his prick straining to stand up at the closeness of Sam's mouth.

"If you try, it messes you up. I shouldn't have said what I did. Will you forgive me?"

"Of course I will." Ruan was going to say *you wazzock*, but decided against it. There were people you could jokingly insult and then there were people who might worry that you meant it, and Sam was very much the second. "D'you forgive me?"

"There's nothing to forgive." Sam tilted his head up so Ruan could see the bright hot gleam in his eye, and moved one of his clinging hands to Ruan's fly button. "I could show you?"

When Ruan tried to imagine it, no matter how much he'd love Sam to suck him off right now, there was a splotch on the corner of his awareness, a darkness he didn't want involved. "Normally I'd be all for it." He smoothed a thumb along Sam's eyebrow and tucked a sprig of hair behind his ear before he drew back and gestured at the plastic bag he'd left outside the circle of the fire. "But not with that thing watching."

"'That thing'?"

Ruan fetched it, decanted it out of its bag and onto the ground without touching it, seeing Sam's expression change from playful to shocked to intrigued. "This thing. It was hanging from my front door this morning."

Sam took the bag from him and thrust his hands into opposite corners, which left him almost gloved up, like someone experimenting with a volatile compound or dangerous virus in a laboratory. He hunkered down over the blood-drenched cloth with a frown and pulled out first one pin and then the other. Seizing the ends of the barbed wire, he unwound them and unwrapped the package they held closed.

Inside was a crow, soggy with blood, and eyeless. Sam exhaled through the nose, a silent laugh, and took the cloth with him to the barrel of rainwater he had set up on one side of the clearing. He put it under the tap, turned the spigot, and watched as cold water sluiced the blood out in a pink torrent that froze when it reached the snow.

"It feels different," he murmured, swallowing, "When it's aimed at you, doesn't it? The intent comes through much more clearly. I hadn't realized."

"It's not aimed at *you*, though," Ruan protested. "It was on *my* door."

"Someone wants us to know that we've seen too much. Or that we need to stop looking."

Sam got that from the missing eyes, probably, but, "I still don't see where you're getting the 'us.'"

Sam smiled, holding up the cloth. Partially cleaned, it was visibly a tea towel, with a picture of the London Eye and a red double-decker bus. "Whoever did this put it on your house to threaten you. But this is *my* tea towel. He must have used it to establish a psychic link between me and the curse—a possession of mine to help it zero in on."

"Where would he even have got that?" Ruan asked, both disturbed at the thought that someone was after Sam too and reassured that they were in this together. "It's not like you've been having house parties."

"No." Sam's pale eyes widened as they sought his in a look of revelation. "But I haven't seen this since the night my laptop was stolen. He must have taken it then."

"You know what that means." Ruan went to sit down on a log, missed it, and ended up froglike on the ground. The new sunshine in his blood gleamed out, sharp and unexpected and glorious, like they'd solved something.

"Yes." Sam's gaze was fond and proud and made him feel like springtime in the middle of the snow. Maybe they were getting somewhere after all. Shut your eyes, be damned. "How likely is it, after all, that we're dealing with two different people here? It's the witch who took my laptop to the caves. But it's the bully who's there now, using his computer to do exactly the same thing—to threaten and frighten people at a distance without revealing his name. And if the bullying and the witchcraft are being done by the same person, if we can solve one, we'll get the other thrown in."

CHAPTER NINETEEN

"Tegan said the witchcraft's been happening awhile too." Ruan's lopsided smirk of pleasure straightened back into a frown. "Someone got a cat like this, long before you arrived. I wasn't listening hard, to be honest. All I really heard was that it couldn't have been you."

Ruan's head was turned away from the crow on its deathbed of linen, though he kept the corner of his eye on it, as though expecting it to hop up to its dead feet and fly at him at any moment. Sam could almost sense him holding himself still against the desire to get away from it, to put miles between them.

Curiously enough, after the first sick blow, the impact of the thing had worn off for Sam. It didn't make him as nervous as a smile he couldn't interpret, or a tone of voice that rang a little out of tune. It was so honest, he didn't have uncertainty enough to feel anxious. He went with some relief straight to anger. How dare this person threaten someone as kind as Ruan? Outrageous!

"Maybe the guy's been caught before, then," he suggested, wondering how to dispose of the curse in a way that would be environmentally friendly and would also neutralize any potential magic on it. "Would there be records in the library?"

Salt was cleansing, wasn't it? Salt and fire. He had those both at hand.

After stripping off his plastic-bag gloves, he went indoors to fetch a candle and a bargain tub of table salt. To the south side of the clearing, a long finger of sunlight had slid beneath the trees and glinted like a knife-edge on the snowy ground. He set the candle up there in its jam-jar holder and lit it with a spill from the fire, then he passed his hands through the smoke of the flame, watching it billow in delicate curlicues through the shaft of light, around the backs of his hands, over his palms, through his fingers, like he was disinfecting them with the light.

"I . . . uh." Ruan had lost his hair-trigger look and stepped closer, apparently forgetting his fear in the light of his curiosity. That was, in fact, three-quarters of the point of this. "Don't think they keep local records there anymore. But it would be like folklore, wouldn't it? So maybe at the institute."

"Institute?" Having purified his hands, Sam built up a lattice of wood in the centre of the fire, into which he dropped the bird, bag and pins, and the blood-soaked cloth on top of all. They both moved away from the smoke that billowed up in a hissing, stinking cloud as a result.

"The Institute of Cornish Culture, on Herriot Street," Ruan clarified, backing off towards the overlap of the windbreak. But before he could get through, the licking flames had dried the towel and Sam had passed a handful of salt through the sun and was beginning to scatter it on top of the fire. Streaks of pure, unnatural blues and greens roared up at every cast, and Sam knew from Ruan's lowered shoulders that the sight of it reassured.

"Shall we go and look when this is burnt?" he asked, wishing for a moment that he could wash the salt and dust off and go back to nuzzling at Ruan's hip, but was pursued by the feeling that everything was picking up speed and he needed to go faster to keep up.

Ruan sighed. "I shouldn't. I still haven't done Alana's and Jennifer's tattoos. So I was going to go get my gun and do that this morning. I've already had my money's worth out of mine. I think they'll want them."

Was he . . . trying to get away, like he had last night? Maybe he didn't want to hang around with Sam anymore. Not after Sam had insulted him like that? He'd seemed reassured—he'd said that Sam was forgiven, but people did say that and then they went on to resent you anyway. Sam bit his lips and tried to work out if *Please don't leave me*, would come across as creepy or clingy or unacceptably desperate. How could he say it in a way that wouldn't make him look like a freak?

"But we'll meet up this evening?"

Ruan's laugh was brightly reassuring, cleansing like the fire. Now that the feathers had singed off the dead bird and its stink receded, Ruan padded back to link his arms around Sam's waist and prop his chin on Sam's shoulder, half friendly, half possessive. Sam's every cell seemed to sigh with relief.

"It won't take me long. We could meet for lunch? At the Hope & Anchor? My treat."

Sam nuzzled Ruan's cheek and sighed as Ruan bent to kiss his neck. "You can't keep feeding me."

"I can." Ruan's mouth moved tantalizingly against the edge of his own. Sam closed his eyes and turned to align them, as Ruan's hands came up to card into his hair, supporting him, reassuring him, not letting him get away.

He didn't want to go anywhere, but give up to the pressure and slide, and the cracking open of something in his chest as burning and as intoxicating as whisky but as sweet as mead.

Ruan disengaged gently, one hand slipping down to curve around the back of his neck as they leaned forehead to forehead, breathing in the warmth of each other's breath.

"I can," Ruan said again. "I can keep feeding you for the rest of your life. I want to see you bloom."

Which was too much. Too much to promise when he probably didn't mean it like that. Too much hope and anguish mixed to hold inside Sam's already aching ribs for any length of time. He let it go before it stung him—too much to ask for. Too much to handle.

"Well, all right. Maybe this time. When I'm rich, I'll pay you back. Two-ish?"

"They stop doing the lunch menu at two." Ruan stepped back as though he knew he was crowding, but his smile was softly happy. "Half one?"

"I'll see you there."

The Institute of Cornish Culture was one of those Victorian re-imaginings of a historical building. Its front occupied almost the whole of Herriot street, opposite a row of tourist shops now shut for the off season. The soaring faux-medieval frontage reminded Sam of the John Rylands Library in Manchester: red brick forced into the ogees and curlicues reminiscent of a stone cathedral.

Sam's inner purist would have liked to disapprove of the raised Book of Kells interlace that flanked the great oak door on both sides, and the church-like stained glass scene of silver-handed Lugh fighting the Dagda that rose above the door and dappled the entrance hall with rainbow spots. It was an anachronistic mix of media and influences that could hardly be said to be authentically Cornish. But even his inner purist had to admit that it was beautiful, and that the inner foyer was a gorgeous space of arched light and peace.

A plump black woman at the entrance desk directed him downstairs to the records department, handing him a card with the passwords on it. "History of local witchcraft?" she repeated at his enquiry, clicking the metal caps of two of her braids together. "Which end d'you want to start at? We've got records going back to the eleventh century, and friends in the press that send us the most recent stuff."

Sam beamed at her nervously. He hated asking people for things, but this was going well. She was certainly acting as though he hadn't interrupted her in the middle of important work—bright and interested and almost as though she didn't mind speaking to him.

"It's not all digitized yet," she went on, with a glance at the floors above, where the floor plan claimed the pick of the collection stood in its museum. "But the most recent stuff is, if that's what you'll want."

"The modern stuff is exactly what I want." He nodded, enthusiastically. Maybe too enthusiastically? He didn't want to come off as a loony, but oh, God, it was so hard. How much was the right amount of gratitude and relief to convey the emotional response expected of him? He always felt like he was getting it wrong. "Starting from now and working back. And as local as possible."

"I can do that," she said. "Come with me, I'll set you up."

The basement was delightfully monastic, held up with fake Norman arches that met in shadowy vaults overhead. The individual cubes for each computer user had a cell-like feel to them, the wooden walls darkly polished around heavy wooden desks. His angel of the institute set him up with a computer, opened tabs to articles sorted by each of the local papers and another sorted by the institute's records by date, and then pointed out the coffee and snacks vending machines and left him to it.

A cursory look at the dates told him a great deal. In 2003, a report of naked shenanigans in Bandry Park had turned out to be a coven who had taken their police warning seriously and clothed themselves thereafter. Their solstice celebration on midwinter and midsummer was now something of a tourist attraction.

Apart from that, the spray-painting of what Sam recognized as a video game logo on a school wall, and a spattering of reports of ghost sightings, there were no occult incidences at all until 2013, when someone received . . . Sam stifled a *Fuck!* There in the crypt-like room, it was obvious that noise was unwelcome, let alone obscenities, but, well, talk about a pattern.

The first incident was of a teenager receiving a parcel that had contained the eyeless body of a dead crow. Posted in Truro—nobody remembered whom by. After that there was an incident almost regularly—every three or four months. Just long enough in between for the papers and any investigators to forget the last one.

They always seemed to feature small animals, though. Sam frowned at the screen, where a picture of a gutted cat in someone's garden, pinned with tent pegs in the centre of a pentacle surrounded by those signature nonsensical symbols, was followed by a shot of a girl in a wheelchair, holding her little sister on her lap and weeping into her hair.

The cruelty of it felt familiar—the petty . . . he could think of no better word for it than *evil*—that desire to hurt someone just because you could. On impulse, he searched on the papers' websites for records of suicide and found more matches than he could tell himself were coincidence.

A fourteen-year-old girl had hanged herself in her bedroom after the death of her pet rat. A twelve-year-old overdosed two days after a bundle had been left on her doorstep.

Sam pushed himself away from the desk and lurched across the floor to the coffee machine, his resilience worn out, his heart heavy and sick and his hands shaking.

He fumbled three times with the plastic cup under the little dispensing alcove before he could get it to stand upright, and he didn't have the mental wherewithal to figure out the glowing icons on the machine's surface. He just stabbed one with his forefinger and told himself he'd regret later the £1.50 he couldn't afford to spend on whatever drink turned up. A tan liquid of some description filled the flimsy white cup to the top, and he looked at it helplessly, already knowing what a disaster it would be if he tried to get it out of its alcove with his hands as they were.

Oh God. Who could do something like this? Who could do this? How could they live with themselves? How could the world permit it? How was it *allowed*?

Someone in a distant cell, hunched in front of their own computer, glared at him as he hyperventilated, and the effect was like a bucket of ice water over his head. He stopped breathing, locked rigid in shock and pain for a moment, and then closed his eyes and dropped everything except for the need to get his own brain back under control.

Concentrate on the breathing, just let it be. Let your awareness dwell within the breath, leaning on the pain in your chest as though you were leaning on a bale of hay, feeling it yield, just slightly, feeling it soften . . .

Gradually he was able to pull the spikes out of his lungs. The long red ache of his spine—knobs like rusted bolts—eased enough to allow him to move. This time when he reached out, he only slopped an inch of liquid into the machine, got the rest of it to his mouth.

The drink was tea, it turned out. Tea with sugar, a whole symphony of bittersweetness in his mouth. It warmed and eased his chest as it went down. With that easing, his mind relaxed enough to let through the observation that Ruan's auntie Jennifer was definitely not this person's usual victim.

This bastard went for teenage girls, not old biddies with shotguns. He went in for softening them up on the computer, targeting their pets, not their livelihood.

So what had changed recently? What had made him single Jennifer out, after all this time on younger prey?

CHAPTER TWENTY

Sam's hands were trembling in his pockets when he slouched out into the cold again and got his phone to direct him to the Hope & Anchor. In the centre of the old town, it was a distinguished-looking coaching inn, several stories high, half-timbered and with the timetable for the stagecoach to London still painted in elegant black penmanship on the white plaster above its door.

Its swinging sign showed a tea clipper with ragged sails being blown towards the rocks, and throwing out a long gold chain attached to a supersized anchor. Presumably there was hope for the vessel if the anchor caught and held on to the sea bottom, keeping her off the teeth of the shore. Or maybe the ship's name had been *Hope*? Ruan would know, if anyone did. It seemed like one of those stories the locals passed down.

He stood beneath the creaking sign for what seemed a long time, as the icy winter wind got its fingers under his collar and spread wings of frost across his back. He didn't want to go in and face the stares of patrons and bar staff alike as he wondered how little he could get away with spending, but it was 1:35 already, and Ruan was probably inside.

Feeling as if he'd had to be brave far too often today, he finally stirred himself to reach out and push the black door open, step inside. For a moment he stood on the gold-and-tan carpet, registering the warmth, the smell of open fires, the glow of a fruit machine to his right, the way three people had raised their heads and locked their gazes on him. And then one of them was standing up and it was Ruan.

Ruan had chosen a small table immediately adjacent to the smaller hearth. The shoulder of his coat was steaming slightly where it draped over his chair. Red napkins under silver cutlery, and Ruan half ran forward to grab Sam's outstretched hands.

"What happened?" Ruan asked, the soft oval of his face drawn for a moment in worry. "Are you all right?"

Sam wrenched his hands back so he could cover his face, but nodded. He could sense the barmaid watching them both, drawing conclusions. He needed to get his act together. This wasn't London, and public displays of affection weren't always safe even there.

"I'm fine," he muttered, shivering, and let Ruan push him over to the seat by the fire and lift the hat off his head. Radiant heat began to knead and massage his sore back, prompting him to take off his coat too and turn himself squarely to the blaze. "I am fine. It just . . . It suddenly got to me. You know? I don't normally believe in the Devil, but you see this and the existence of absolute evil becomes . . . viscerally real, you know?"

"I do." Ruan sat opposite him, soft despite his beaky nose—soft brown eyes; soft, ruffled hair; and that well-fed hint of sleekness on top of the raw bones of his face. "What did you find?"

Sam took the folded menu and let himself be jarred out of thoughts of good and evil by the contemplation of fish gazey pie, battered halloumi, or steak and ale savoury crumble with stilton topping. "I'm more sure than ever that there's only one person involved here. I don't exactly have proof, but the . . ." he made a gesture intended to convey the concept of piecing together a single picture out of a jigsaw of tiny parts, "the grammar of both things seems to be the same. If you know what I mean?"

"I don't." Ruan made eye contact with the barmaid, a young woman with startlingly blue, green, and purple hair that must have been like a distant nebula before it grew out far enough for the mousy roots to show. She picked up a notepad and came over. "But if you say it, I believe it. Anyway, the tattoos are done. I think Alana's secretly thrilled—thinks it makes her a bad girl and all." He grinned up at the barmaid. "Two pints of the Doom Bar, please, Gloria, and I'll have the scampi."

Sam didn't want to be reminded of dead animals right now, so he ordered the battered halloumi and chips. The fat would do him good, anyway.

"Be about half an hour," Gloria said, touching her notepad to her tawny lips. In contrast with her short-wavelength hair, her makeup was all oranges and golds. "Is that okay?"

The excuse to sit quietly in front of the fire for half an hour was welcome.

"No problem," Ruan said. He grinned and stretched out his foot beneath the table so he could graze his toe up Sam's calf, beaming with achievement when Sam smiled back.

"Anyway." Sam pretended his flush was from the fire and carried on. "What it amounts to is some bastard who gets a power kick out of literally frightening young girls to death. I would have almost said that Jennifer's problem was an isolated incident. Someone else, I mean. Except that the symbols he used around the sheep were exactly the same as the ones around Mary Nowell's pet cat. It's the same person, then, but whatever he's doing with Jennifer is . . . different? I don't know. It doesn't fit."

It was so hard to hold on to the horrifying revelation of how awful people could be, here in the cheerful warmth with Ruan across the table, sprawled like a dozing panther, wearing a gaze that was half *rub my belly*, half *I'm going to eat you up*. Sam was glad of the beer's arrival to wet his suddenly dry throat.

Ruan's earring was a ruby today, like an ember in the smoke of his hair. This small fact meant a lot to Sam, though he couldn't have said why.

Ruan caught him staring at it and smiled. "Why don't you ask the cards?" he said. "They did us right the last time."

That was not a bad idea. The tarot was still in the pocket of his coat from when he'd rushed to get them at Jennifer's. He pulled the pack out and fanned them face up on the table, letting them warm up and absorb the aura of the place, while he considered which spread to use.

"Can you read them things?" Having brought the beers on a small black tray, Gloria canted it on her hip and peered at the jewel-bright pictures of Sam's Wild Wood deck in fascination.

Sam opened his mouth in preparation to say, *Anybody can. There's nothing particularly magical about it. It's purely a way of getting you in touch with your own intuition.* But as he was martialling this sentence into order, Ruan got in first.

"Course he can," he said, openly proud. "He's a white wizard. He's like Merlin. Even lives up in a grove, in a hermitage, like a proper holy man."

Sam curled over the embers that put in his stomach—glowing embers of embarrassment, but also of delight. Ruan really genuinely liked him, didn't he? He wasn't putting it on—not if he'd expose his ridiculous partiality and faith in public like this. The warmth of the thought drove the last of the cold straight out of him, left him aglow. He was now in a different, more intense universe than he'd ever lived in before.

He still wasn't sure he would ever have the nerve to look up again.

"Is that so?" Gloria was saying, apparently impressed. "That's why he's shy, is it?" And a shift in some indefinable way that made it clear she was suddenly talking to him. "You don't need to be shy, mister. You can tell my fortune. I'll pay you, if you're that good."

That thought startled him enough to raise his eyes and catch her gaze. It was half jokey and half genuinely nervous. She looked fascinated and a little afraid, and deep down he thought that also she was probably only trying to help him. For all there was evil here that had turned Sam's stomach, there also seemed to be more good than he had allowed himself to expect from the world, and he didn't want to let it down.

"I'm not sure I ought to be paid."

"Course you should," she insisted. "You do a job of work you deserve to be paid. That's only right. You're serious about this, though?"

He picked the pack up, remembering what it had felt like when it was new and stiff. There'd been a lot of readings since then, teaching himself with the guidance of free books and long, empty, lonely evenings. The cards were softer now, fitted to his hands, and part of his thinking in a way he could no longer separate from the normal workings of his mind. "Yes," he agreed. "It's part of the architecture of the world for me."

Gloria cut her eyes sideways to Ruan, who smiled as if he'd said something profound. "I see what you mean. Look, if you're not happy about money, why don't you do this and I'll sub you lunch?"

Sam had started to come round to the idea of money, to the thought of being able to afford to run the van's heater for a while and take his bedclothes to the launderette, but it was too late to say so now. "Thank you," he said. "Are there any specific questions you wanted answered, or do you want a general reading of where you are and what might be in store?"

"I'll see what you've got to say." She dragged a third chair over and sank into it, keeping one eye on the empty bar, the other on the pack in his hands. *Shrewd*, he thought, giving him no hint of what to look for. This would be a genuine test. He would go for the Celtic Cross spread, because it was appropriate to the setting, and it was aesthetically pleasing, and it would introduce enough complexity to be sure he was getting *something* right no matter what.

Her scientific detachment didn't last long. By the time the lunches came, they were into the nitty-gritty of choosing colleges, wondering whether to leave a boyfriend behind or to stay close for his sake.

"This says change—remaking," Sam admitted, gesturing to the Death card. "The end of one life and the beginning of a new. And then these further cards are very positive—increased connection with the universe and with yourself. A new strength or power. I don't know what you wanted, but . . ."

A moment's pause in which he had time to regret he'd ever spoken, and then she was beaming at him and hugging him over the empty remains of his bucket of chips. He gave an inward sigh even as he cringed away from more personal contact than he was comfortable with. Oh, it was a relief when the cards supported what the person already wanted to do.

"That's brilliant." Gloria stacked their empty dishes like she was already packing to leave. "I won't feel so bad now, doing what I have to. Here, if you change your mind about reading these for money, I can send quite a few people up your way. That Holly in the kitchen? She's got to make a decision about selling her house; she's been worrying about it for months now. You'd be doing her a favour, really."

The thought of it was increasingly attractive. He caught Ruan's eye and watched the edge of it crinkle as he smiled. "If I could make a bit of money, I could afford to stay. I could pay Jennifer a little rent for the copse, and keep warm. Buy food."

Ruan's grin was radiant as a new moon, actually pleased at the prospect of him staying, and it felt claustrophobic and terrifying and utterly, unbearably wanted, to know that Ruan was imagining a future with him in it.

"You totally should." Ruan rose. He went to fling his scarf on as usual, then hesitated. With a smile of shy mischief, he lifted it over Sam's head instead, wrapping it twice around Sam's neck like he was trying to wrap up an awkward parcel. His happiness seemed to flow out of him and light Sam's face and rusted-up spine with a more golden heat than the fire in the hearth. The wool was even warmer, faintly scratchy, enveloping Sam in Ruan's scent. Sam caught both ends of the scarf in his hands and raised them to his face, breathing in, touched to the point of tears.

"We should work together," Ruan was saying, his smile broadened into another huge proud grin. "I've been thinking about this, in fact. I can do magic-charged tattoos and you can give people advice. IT things. Tarot readings, whatever. People'd lap that stuff up. 'Specially if they had to go, like, to a sacred grove to get it."

This only confirmed that Ruan was a big black dog of a man. One who'd just heard the word *walkies* and now couldn't get out the door fast enough. Sam didn't know if he was ready to be tied down like this—wanted to think about business licences and taxes and not be swept away by an enthusiasm that might wane in a couple of weeks and leave them in a worse mess. But he also didn't want to disappoint Ruan, and he could do with bringing in some money if he was to stay here and allow this almost impossible future a chance.

"Come on." Ruan took him by the elbow and tugged him back out into the cold. "I know just where we can start getting the word out."

CHAPTER TWENTY-ONE

On the edge of the multistorey car park was a portacabin on the side of which Sam read the words *Porthkennack Gazette*. As offices went, this was considerably less intimidating than the kind he'd fled from, and he felt barely a twinge of terror as he opened the door and led Ruan through. Inside, someone had attempted to add a festive air to the scuffed laminate and plastic of the front room by putting up a pale-blue plastic Christmas tree in a red plastic pot next to the kettle and decorating it in balding tinsel. It didn't convince.

The only other thing in the tiny room was a desk heaped high with eclectic envelopes, on which the monitor of an all-but-obsolete PC was raised to eye level on a stack of glossy magazines. Additional tinsel had been Blu-Tacked around its screen. Presumably by the middle-aged lady who was sitting in a plastic garden chair behind the desk, trying to talk into two phones at once.

"I thought you said you had a puppet show? Cancelled? And the wreath-making workshop's cancelled too? Listen, I need something to make this sound good. Have you got anything that makes this event more interesting than a regular Sunday car-boot sale?"

In front of Ruan and Sam, a tall, thin woman was slowly drooping around her armful of folders.

"Are those for the paper?" The woman on the phones covered both mouthpieces briefly and indicated a shoe box on the desk, which appeared to be full of torn-out pages from notebooks, ideas scribbled on napkins, and earnest essays on A4 paper. "Your phone number on them?"

Droopy nodded.

"Just put them in the in-box there and I'll get back to you."

With an air of relief, the woman balanced her folders on top of the shoe box and nodded to Ruan furtively as she went out, brushing past Sam as if she didn't see him.

The woman on the phones had a suspiciously beaky nose, made harsher by her buzz-cut black hair. She wore a Truro United football jumper and a pair of pink-and-grey combat trousers with pink Doc Martens.

"That's my cousin Sue," Ruan leaned in to whisper to him. "She's my mam's brother's second youngest. She pretty much runs this paper single-handed."

"Perfect. I'll call round for an interview in person tomorrow." One phone went down, and Sue took the time to wave at Ruan before sighing into the other. "How am I supposed to make this sound like it's worth going to if all your entertainers have cancelled? No, it's not my business to write some puff piece to sell it for you. I report on what you tell me, I don't make stuff up." Another deeper sigh and then, "Well, I suppose the cake stall was good last year. And the samba band is still booked? I'll think of something."

The second phone clicked into its cradle. Sue stretched, showing toned and sun-bed orange arms, her sleeves shoved up past her elbow. "All right, Ruan," she said, getting up to fill the kettle from a plastic bottle of water and put it on. "Who's your friend?"

"This is Sam Atkins." Ruan smiled at Sam, probably in an attempt to reassure him that Sue's gimlet gaze was not going to literally pierce and shred him. Sam backed off anyway, sidling away with his back to the wall until he could see the computer monitor and the half-filled-in layout of a page that occupied it.

"Sam's living up in Foxglove Copse," Ruan went on, trailing him a couple of steps behind as though he wanted to touch but didn't quite have the nerve. "He's got an eco-warrior setup up there. I thought maybe you could do an article about him. Sustainable living, like."

"I could." Sue's expression sharpened even further as she brought a vape pen out of her desk drawer and lit it up. Twin clouds of steam— one smelling of menthol—helped explain the black mould spots on the ceiling. "Why would he want me to, though?"

That sounded like an opportunity to sell himself. A wave of memory and sickness rolled over Sam at the thought. Too many pitch meetings, business meetings, five-year plans, PowerPoint presentations behind him, where he stared at his shiny shoes and wanted to die. He grimaced, studying the computer screen rather than meeting anyone's gaze.

"Well," Ruan spoke for him as he puzzled out the picture in the middle of the screen. Some sort of plan. Houses—lots of little houses? He scanned the text.

"Sam's a bit of a mystic and a good witch. He gets by with reading people's fortunes in the tarot—advising them on their life decisions, that kind of thing. So I told him maybe you'd put something in about that, so people would know who to come to and what his rates were and how to find him."

"Without having to pay to take out an advert, you mean." Sue crossed her arms and exhaled clouds.

Apparently a local council member had proposed this plan for a new holiday camp, featuring a hundred thirty-two self-catering chalets and a central hub containing a swimming pool, cinema, and rental space for local restaurants and craft stores. It would bring millions into the local economy, or so it claimed, with no damage to wildlife or the existing infrastructure of the town.

That sounded rather too good to be true. Where would they put it, for a start?

"We don't have much money."

Sam glanced up in time to see Ruan tilt his head to one side and give his cousin the lopsided, roguish smile that Sam found so charming. Apparently he wasn't the only one.

"But it would be an interesting article. 'Techno-mage speaks up about local occultism'—that would work too."

"*Can* he speak?" Sue asked, and even with his nose pressed to the computer to read the small print of the article, he knew she was watching him again. "Wait a minute. Did you say tarot readings? Like a cross-my-palm-with-silver–and-I'll-tell-you-the-future deal?"

It wasn't anything like that, but the two of them were so far away in their bubble of easy family companionship that Sam didn't feel able to say so. And, anyway, was he reading this correctly?

"Well, it's a bit more attuning with cosmic forces, I think." Ruan gave a doubtful shrug. "But, basically, yes."

"'Cause I happen to know that the Hotel Metropole on the seafront is gagging for entertainers for its Christmas Fayre after half the ones they had booked have cancelled. Likewise, I need something new to say about the whole affair. I could phone 'em up dreckly, and I bet they'd book him in this minute. If he does talk, that is."

They both turned to look at Sam. He felt it keenly—like being observed on the other end of a telescope, like he was a long way away on an alien planet. Or they were.

Then Ruan smiled again, this one big and soppy and indulgent. "He's like he's got one foot in fairyland, you know? Like he's too special for this world. But he knows what he's doing, certain sure, if you sit him down and put the cards in front of him."

"Oh." Sue snorted like a dragon, her bony face unexpectedly soft. "Oh, lover, I see how it is. And since it's for you . . ."

Sam hugged himself. He didn't agree, of course. It was obvious that Ruan was the wild creature, the thing on the cusp of fantasy, with his ridiculous fancies and his childlike faith, but how . . . how . . . His eyes stung briefly, and he closed them to be sure they didn't leak. How nice to be thought of as something rare and miraculous, instead of something weak.

"I'll call them up now."

Sam refocussed on the screen. It claimed the article continued over the next page. Without thinking, he reached out and clicked. The map was instantly recognizable—the standing stone known as Sir Richard, the circle in which he'd found the first sheep, the dark-green blur of the copse he was beginning to think of as home. "This is Jennifer's land. How could they build a holiday camp there? Is she selling up?"

Ruan's easy slouch stiffened like he'd met the eyes of Medusa. He broke out of it fast afterwards, but not before Sam had seen, and knew he'd put his prying nose in something important.

"A holiday camp?" Now Ruan's smile was all teeth, his eyes full of dread above it. He swooped close as Sam paged back to the beginning of the article for him. "Let me see."

"Well they can't build it there unless Jennifer sells 'em the land." Sue, too, was watching Ruan with concern as he read, his fingers curling white round the edge of the desk and the muscles of his cheek rigid as he clenched his jaw. "Which, yeah, I was surprised to see it too. That was leaked to me from a local council meeting. It's only a proposal at present. I've been debating about whether to put it in the paper or not. People deserve to be told, but it'd lay a deal of pressure on Jennifer to sell up. You know? If everyone and their dog was thinking she was the only thing in the way of jobs for their kids and grandkids. If she thinks she's hampering her nephews and nieces' futures, she might be persuaded maybe?"

"If she thinks the land is cursed," Ruan whispered, turning to Sam as if for reassurance, for guidance. "If she thinks she can't live there safely anymore."

"You think it's connected with the curses?" Sam's rational mind told him not to jump to conclusions, but his intuition was there already. This fitted with what the cards had said—a monetary motive, driving forces of greed and materialism, not spirituality, however dark.

Ruan shook his head, his eyes wide and almost luminous in their certainty. "I *know* it is. I've seen this plan before. When I went to visit Grandma Wyn, it was up on her laptop with costings and graphs and so on. More detailed than this. Planned out further."

"Oh don't." Sue switched the screen off, pushed Ruan on the shoulder, and made a shooing gesture towards Sam. "Don't. I don't want to hear it. I can't report on anything I don't know, so whatever you're talking about, take it away."

"It's, uh—" Ruan started, only to be halted with a spread palm in the centre of his chest. Sue's black-winged eyes were trying to convey some urgent message to Ruan without involving Sam, but Sam could guess by now. *Not in front of outsiders.*

"No," she said firmly to Ruan, turning to Sam to continue. "I'll book you in for this fair and write up a piece that'll bring some business to the copse, but I don't want to be messed up in whatever this is. You should drop it too."

"But Jennifer—"

"Jennifer is a tough old bird, and she can look after herself. We'll be behind whatever she chooses to do all the way, but we are not going head-to-head with," she lowered her voice, perhaps in the hope that Sam wouldn't hear it, "the Lusmoores. Now get out of here. I've work to do."

Ruan held her eye a moment more and then slumped, looking so defeated that Sam took his hand, twining their fingers together and squeezing.

"Please," he said, letting some of his discomfort show, "let's just leave."

Outside, the short afternoon was damp but milder than it had been, bringing a quiet softness to the dripping gutters of the car park and the distant roars of manoeuvring vehicles. Even from here in the middle of the peninsula, there was a faint stir and brightness to the sky that reflected a distant sea. It felt good to Sam, for whom the tangles of the past weeks were smoothing beneath his mental fingers as he finally loosened and picked apart the knot.

For lack of any other instruction, he began to walk back towards his van, Ruan falling into place at his side like an overly casual bodyguard. "So let me get this straight," Sam started, recapping because it soothed him to be able to get things out there, in order, bugs removed, logic moving on from one step to another like water falling gently down a weir. "The Lusmoores are your local crime family?"

"They've been pirates, smugglers, and wreckers as long as there was a sea to bring them prey." Ruan sighed, looking worried by his own words. "Some of them've been heroes too, mind. I'm not saying they're all bad. I'm not saying the other families are all good, neither. Just . . ."

Sam nodded, understanding that he was not being called on for blanket condemnation. "Of course. I'm not saying that either. But what we do have is proof that a campaign of bullying is being carried out by someone with an IP address in a Lusmoore warehouse. Strong circumstantial evidence suggests the same person has been waging psychological warfare on local teenagers through . . . ugh. I'm going to call it 'witchcraft' for lack of a better word, though I strongly suspect it isn't, not really."

Ruan nodded.

"This goes on for years," Sam continued, "with no apparent goal other than to hurt vulnerable young girls seemingly for the thrill of it. If I was to guess, I would imagine the culprit was a disaffected teenager himself, striking out at his classmates to make him feel big."

They turned a corner into the high street, where neon candlesticks on the lampposts vied with multicoloured fairy-light angels, pale as luminous fish, since sunlight lingered in the sky.

"But then Grandma Wyn comes into the picture," Sam mused, not quite believing this Mafia nonsense. "And she wants to build on Jennifer's land. She knows Jennifer won't agree to sell up if she just asks. So she sets our bully on her. That explains why Jennifer isn't one of his normal victims—why he's broken his pattern—because someone else is now using him for their own purposes. So I think that although it's unlikely your clan matriarch is doing this herself, she absolutely knows who is, and is encouraging him. I think the next step is to get the police to look into her."

Ruan stopped. In the shop window behind him, polished teak ship wheels gleamed with brass among ship bells and sextants, ornamental nets, striped, nautical sweaters, and matching his and hers hats that read *Captain* and *First Mate*. For all that he was supposed to be the mystic of the pair, for all his words about clan matriarchs and their putting to use the monsters in their family, Sam was struggling with the idea that Cornish piracy still existed—was neither fictional nor as romantic as he had always believed.

Which didn't stop him taking a frivolous moment to picture Ruan in breeches and sea boots, his long hair tied back in a tail beneath a tricornered hat, like someone out of *Treasure Island*. He'd be the young innocent, though, the good-hearted young man who only wanted to help his mother pay off her taxes or run her inn.

But Ruan was shaking his head now. "No. No. You can't call the police on Grandma Wyn. If you did, they wouldn't go. All the families've got people on their ships. All the local businesses belong to them or owe them or trade with them. Besides, you *can't*. Local business is between the locals. You can't make it official. You'd disappear in the middle of the night and no one would think twice about where you'd gone. No. I'm going to have to handle this myself."

He'd gone almost grey. His hand in Sam's was icy cold and shaking, and that was so wrong—it made Sam so angry—that he was able to shove away his onrushing demon of fear, at least for the moment. He nudged Ruan's shoulder and, when Ruan looked down at him, said, "But not on your own. What if we caught him red-handed? You and me and Jennifer? What if we staked out Jennifer's land and, when he tried again, we got proof we could show to the girls and their parents? What if we could let everyone know who he was? Not the police, per se, but everyone else?"

Ruan's trembling worsened, but his white face broke into a smile of terrified glee. "They do say that evil can't abide being dragged out into the light, don't they? And I owe it to Tegan. I owe it to myself. I'm fed up of being scared of them. Let's do it!"

CHAPTER
TWENTY-TWO

For the next ten nights they became nocturnal. Ruan brought his father's binoculars and Jimmy's telescope with him, and they sat as high as they could safely climb in the tallest oak at the edge of the coppice, sweeping the fields for any sign of movement. Jennifer's number on speed dial, and the farmhouse's outside lights all switched on, casting some illumination out into the bunched hills.

After the first four hours of the first night, in which the only moving things were the charcoal clouds streaming up from the sea, Ruan felt himself slip into another world. He'd been hot with the need to do something. Hot with fury and yet burning cold with fear. Torn, like, and instinctual, all taken up with fight-or-flight hind-brain urgency. But as they gazed into the night together, patient, Sam talking about his months on the road, Ruan coming back with tales of local history, sharing the steam of their breath, one or the other getting down every couple of hours to make tea, Ruan had felt himself easing into quiet. Almost into meditation.

He knew he was fanciful. He'd be the first to laugh in self-defence if anyone ever got out of him the things he was thinking. But this was—it really was like going on his own vision quest, preparing himself like a medieval knight praying in the sanctuary all night before a single combat. He honest to God did feel like the night and the cold and the great sky were shaping him to be a hero. When they stumbled to bed in the scraped pewter light of the dawn and lay there for hours in and out of sleep, kissing as they tried to get warm, even that felt holy too.

He'd lie abed while the sun rose, watching Sam's face soft with sleep and rejoice in the faint suggestion that his cheeks were rounder, his bones better padded than the first time they'd lain entwined.

Later in the day they'd stir awake gradually, already touching everywhere, and make love, then lie in the comfort of their own warmth, Sam's head on Ruan's arm or chest, and talk again.

A couple of times the girls came back, one or the other of them with a letter from their mam giving them permission to have the tattoo. So Ruan did three more of those, all told. And on the day after the *Gazette* came out, two people came up to have their fortunes told. Sam tucked forty quid into his wallet with a dazed expression that Ruan had to kiss away, it looked so forlorn.

By the start of the tenth night, Ruan would have been happy if this little interlude outside the rest of the world could have gone on forever. Perhaps that was why the tenth night was the night when it all changed.

It was a clear night, the stars piercing above as though the round world was their pincushion. By now Ruan knew all the hollows of the land like the hollows of his own palm. He knew what the sheep looked like, drowsing, and the rabbits and the badgers out nibbling grass and worm. He still imagined the shadow was a cloud at first—a long finger of it, wavering as it went east to west through the lights of the house. *Not a human shape*, he thought as he tried to eke more magnification out of his binoculars while his heart raced up to speed and his hands and feet stung with pins and needles as they grew suddenly warm.

He caught Sam's elbow and pointed. "D'you see it?"

Sam had been sweeping the other side of the headland. Now he carefully wriggled closer so he could train his telescope in the right direction. There was a long moment while he peered through, and then a hiss, sibilant and smug. "That's him. It has to be. He has a sack on his back, and it's dripping."

"I'll call Jennifer." Ruan did just that, paranoid that the distant bent-over figure would hear him. Jennifer picked up after the first ring, from where she was sitting up in the attic, keeping a watch out with her own binoculars or maybe the sight of a rifle.

"Ruan?"

"He's here, Auntie. He's heading to Dickie." Ruan backtracked along the way the figure seemed to have come and found a white Fiat parked in a passing place just outside Jennifer's fence. "His car's up by the Maddingly Road."

"I'm going to get him."

Sam had been listening in, his head touching Ruan's. Even in the dark his hair was shadowed gold. "Tell her we need proof first. We'll get closer and record what the guy is doing on our phones. Jennifer should do the same. Tell her not to confront the guy until we're all there. He killed two sheep with a chainsaw, remember? Best to assume he's dangerous."

Hearing Sam's calm, clipped voice next to him, so collected and sensible, Ruan felt his fear and excitement melt into exaltation. Who the hell'd managed to convince Sam he couldn't get anything right? Sam was amazing.

"I thought you had an anxiety problem," he muttered as they climbed down the tree and made their way easily—in the starlight, with their dark-adapted eyes—out towards the phallic standing stone.

"I do," Sam hissed back, and indeed his pale eyes looked faintly manic with that off-kilter smile. "Fortunately I don't seem to be able to believe that this is really happening. Try not to mention it again, though, please? If I think about it too much, I might have a panic attack."

As they crossed the figure's path, Ruan's boot came down in something that squelched. Sam made a gulping retch of a sound as the smell hit Ruan's nose. Not the meaty, coppery smell of blood, but much worse—sweet decay and crawling things and faecal slime, and his autonomic nervous system told him he should run away fast.

He didn't. He lurched two steps forward and hugged Sam tight, and somehow what they had between them—that pure unconsuming fire—drove the darkness back out. "Shit," he gasped, his hands petting Sam's back, soothing Sam's trembling. "I don't like that smell."

"No." Sam's breath was rapid and shallow and his grip was going to leave bruises on Ruan's arms, but he pressed his forehead into Ruan's neck and whispered calming nonsense to himself until he could continue. "But we'd better follow the trail. Try not to be seen."

Keeping low, they followed the wet stench up to the brow of the hill and lay down there flat. Ruan fumbled his good camera out of his coat, framed the figure by the stone in his viewfinder and hit Record, while Sam did the same with his phone.

Though the starlight was bright enough so he could see the shapes of individual boulders and trees, he still had to squint hard at the moving black blur that was their quarry. Something about him did look familiar. Something about the way he moved, maybe? It was a him, certainly—tall and shaven-headed, hatless even in the cold.

The man laid his bag down beneath the standing stone, spreading it out until it laid flat against the ground. A smallish lump gleamed as he picked it up and checked it, and a larger lump next to it had the straight-sided contours of some kind of machine. That would be the chainsaw.

Ruan's phone vibrated in his pocket, thankfully distracting him from thoughts of the chainsaw.

Recording him now.

That was Jennifer, in place, hopefully close. Probably had Tiger with her. Ruan squirmed forward on his belly to get a better view as the still frustratingly anonymous man got his shoulder beneath the third lump and pushed it up against the stone. Not the right shape for a sheep, the third lump was . . . another scarecrow?

The *crack* of a nail gun, one-two-three-four in rapid succession, almost covered up the disturbing squelch of the man's movements as he nailed the figure's arms to a plank. The standing stone already bore another rope collar around its top, and now the witch was lifting the plank and hooking it on with meathooks, so that the scarecrow hung as if crucified.

It was a convincing scarecrow. Ruan snaked closer, scarcely aware that he had left his heart and stomach behind him. It looked just like . . .

Oh fucking— Fucking—

He had to fight the involuntary surge of his whole body, swallowing down bile as he refused to throw up. *Fucking Christ have mercy.*

Not a scarecrow at all. The ghoul had escalated his tactics again. This was— Ruan couldn't look. No, but he had to. He had to take footage, because this was Linda, the girl they'd buried only a fortnight ago, swollen now and leaking in her stained satin shroud, and Ruan couldn't feel his own face, had no idea he was standing up, sprinting forward to attack until his shoulder connected with the man's back.

The great jarring blow sent his opponent flying, but knocked Ruan away too as his senses suddenly caught up with him.

"Ruan!" Sam yelled, scrambling to his own feet, lit strangely from beneath by the light of his phone screen. Ruan swayed on his feet, still wanting to throw up, wanting to run to Sam, not knowing how to follow up his impulsive charge. And in that moment the man grabbed up his chainsaw and yanked the cord.

"No!" Sam's panicked scream was high-pitched enough to pierce the clamour of the blades turning. He started forward just as the baying of an angry dog heralded Tiger streaking into the clearing like a black-and-white comet. Tiger went straight for the stranger's legs. The man turned and slashed out with the saw at the same time that Tiger jumped for his face.

Ruan saw it in slow motion. It was the jump that saved the dog. The saw would have come down on his backbone if he hadn't already been leaping up. As it was, it passed mostly beneath him. Ruan thought everything was going to be all right, but then the dog's momentum brought it down out of its arc, the man pulled the blade back, and the tip bit into Tiger's rib cage and flung him across the hollow to lie motionless and whimpering.

As the witch turned to watch the dog's fall, a rising moon lit his face in shades of milk, and Ruan went cold all over again. Because this wasn't a man at all. It was Clem Lusmoore. In his final year at school, the acne not yet dried from his face, he was only a boy and already damned.

"I see you. I see you, Clem Lusmoore. You're going to pay for all of this." Even the words didn't feel like Ruan's own, bursting out of him as if inspired, as he ran too hot with fury to mind the bloodied saw.

"You come any closer, you can have some of this too." Clem flourished the chainsaw at him like a battleaxe, his eyes wide with the terrified anger of something backed into a trap. Behind Ruan, Sam circled around to fall to his knees by Tiger. Auntie Jennifer grabbed Sam's wrists, made him push down on Tiger's wound, then Jennifer was standing, outside Clem's eyeline, her shotgun pulled up to her cheek.

"I'm not scared of you," Ruan told Clem, keeping him distracted, fixated on Ruan. Except that he *was* scared, somewhere in the shrillness of his bones, somewhere in the back of his mind—he really was. What was Jennifer planning? She wouldn't murder the boy, surely?

Clem's blotchy face twisted into a slightly theatrical smile. He took a step forward, feinting with the blade again—a taunt, not a genuine attempt to connect. "You are, little fag. You are afraid of me, and if you aren't, you should be."

He lunged. Ruan leapt back as the hills echoed with the *crack-boom* of the shotgun. Both slugs slammed into the buzzing body of the saw. The engine choked out as shrapnel flew. With a sharp bark of pain and rage, Clem threw the useless machine down and looked around wildly. "That's not fair! This is my game. You don't get to—" He cut himself off, gesturing angrily.

Sam, on his knees by Tiger, was just holding on to the dog's life, head down. The camera in Ruan's left hand was still recording, and his right was in a fist so tight it ached. Clem choked back the remainder of his sentence and made a tentative step towards the nail gun just as Jennifer brought her hand out of her pocket with two more slugs and slid the first into the barrel.

Something about Clem's stance said *Darth Vader* as he stopped and turned back towards Ruan—as though he was mimicking the grandiose villain to make him feel untouchable. "You don't know what you've done, Gwynn. You've doomed everyone you care for." Clem put his head down and charged straight at Ruan.

Sidestepping the charge, Ruan threw a punch, but Clem caught his wrist in a two-handed grip, twisted, and slipped beneath Ruan's arm. Before Ruan knew what was happening, he'd been thrown onto his back and Clem was running. Getting away.

Still on autopilot, full of righteousness, Ruan rolled to his feet and followed.

CHAPTER TWENTY-THREE

The car, Ruan thought, head down with his thigh muscles aching from running flat out. If he could keep between Clem and the car, they'd have him in the end. And the car should go to the police—fuck keeping this private among the locals now. Clem had crossed a line.

Ruan had never really been a physical person, too busy with extra art classes, with reading and exploring every gallery and bookshop-art-history section to go in for exercise, but his genes had done him a favour; he was big and long-legged and broad. When he threw himself at Clem's retreating knees, the shock of the impact brought Clem down, sprawling in the wet tussocks, thistles, and sheep shit of the field.

The earlier throw had half convinced him that Clem had martial arts training. Ruan expected to be kicked off and karate chopped in no time flat, but Clem lay dazed against the ground for long enough for Ruan to climb up his body, hand over hand, and settle his weight in the middle of Clem's back.

"I'll . . ." Clem wheezed—the fall must have winded him. But he still seemed fully committed to his evil-overlord act. "I'll make you pay for this. You don't know what powers I have, what kind of creatures I've got on my leash. Demons, Ruan Gwynn." He giggled, and despite himself Ruan felt the hair raise itself up on the back of his neck. "Oh, terrible things they are. Terrible things they're going to do to you and yours, from your little faggot friend to your tranny sister."

Ruan hadn't done much fighting in his life, didn't know how to throw a punch scientifically, but it was like his arm moved by itself, drawing back and wellying Clem with a hard smack, open-handed across the ear. Fuck! That hurt! The bones in Ruan's hand felt like they'd exploded, then rebounded back together with a red bursting sting.

Clem howled and bucked up, throwing Ruan upward, and twisted so that when Ruan came down, it was onto Clem's belly rather than his back. As he considered going in for the other ear, or a punch to the nose—that would hurt worse, surely?—Clem seized his duffle coat by both lapels. Jerking Ruan forward, Clem surged up to meet him. Ruan was still trying to work out what exactly was happening, when the hard bone of Clem's forehead slammed into the bridge of his nose.

Whiteout and agony. He wasn't even in his body for a moment, and when he dropped back into it, it was to find himself on his side on the wet ground, curled around a nest of swirling grey stars, his head bursting and his guts roiling like a boiling pan.

"You think you can find me? You won't ever find me again. But I'll find you."

Ruan pushed himself up to his hands and knees. This time he couldn't fight the urge as his body spasmed, ribs locking hard, forcing him to throw up his dinner in a warm flood over his hands.

Clem laughed above him, and as he shook, cold, wrung out and at the mercy of the vice that was crushing his head, he felt Clem's hands pat down his pockets. Ruan made a weak grab for his camera as Clem drew it from his coat. Then it was thrown down next to him, and Clem's foot came down on the lens and drove it through the body of the camera, shattering both and grinding the pieces under his heel.

That had been a birthday present, that had. The whole family'd chipped in for it, it had been so expensive. The memory chip was full of art references and special moments spent with friends. "You . . ." Ruan staggered to his feet, wondering what the hell was keeping Jennifer; a shotgun would come in handy now. "You bastard. You won't get away. We've got the registration of your car. There'll be DNA in there. You must have put her in the boot, right?" A sob forced its way out of him unexpectedly as he swayed. "How could you? You couldn't even let her rest in peace?"

Clem laughed again, stretched out a slow hand and shoved him in the centre of the chest, sending him reeling away. Ruan caught himself before he fell on his arse, and fought the urge to close his eyes as everything around him gave a sickening dizzy swirl.

"It's not my car, you wazzock." He could hear Clem smiling now, enjoying his moment in the spotlight. "You think I'd be that stupid? I don't need a car to disappear into thin air. I'm telling you, I've got powers you wouldn't believe. I've got friends in very low places indeed."

Ruan thought of the Devil card, that grinning face, tusked and horned like a ram, surrounded by the lake of fire. It made him shake. But this was Clem Lusmoore, who'd always been a lying little toad. Clem, who thought he was too manly for deodorant. Ruan would like to think the Devil was enough of a gentleman to want nothing to do with the likes of Clem.

Anyway, Sam didn't believe in all of that, and Sam should know. "Sure," he said, dragging the word out to make his scepticism crystal clear. "Sure you do. Prove it."

He did honestly think for a moment that Clem's face was glowing an eerie red, but no, that was just the change of light in the east as dawn lifted a red ember over the horizon. Clem met his gaze for a moment, grey-green eyes snapping with bravado.

But there was terror under it. Ruan just caught sight of a fleeting glimpse of humanity like Clem was scaring himself too, when Clem stormed forward, grabbed him by the hair—nearly tearing a handful out—and overbalanced him backwards, throwing him to the ground. The toe of Clem's boot kicked into the bruise between Ruan's eyebrows, setting off another sleet of stars, making him curl away and throw up a second time, miserable and sightless.

When he could force himself to look up again, Clem was gone.

Ruan grabbed at the earth to try to stop it from swinging about so he could stand up, got himself to hands and knees and then to a crouch and peered over to the parked car. Maybe if he pushed himself . . . If he could get his legs to stop shaking, he could run, catch up with Clem before he got there, try this whole thing again.

But Clem wasn't making for the car. Dawn's dim light was now broad enough that Ruan could see it, peacefully parked in the lay-by, rust or blood streaks down its boot. But no Clem. No sight of him walking the bare hills. He couldn't have got to the copse yet, couldn't have got to any cover. Whether he was loping away or lying down hoping not to be seen, he should still be clearly visible from here.

For a moment, Ruan felt a borehole open in the centre of him and let in a rising pressure of black, freezing fear. What if it was true, though? What if Clem Lusmoore had honest to God made a deal with the Devil, the way he'd been careful to make it look like he had. What would a little git like him do with a power like that?

Ruan looked back at the standing stone, where the swollen dead body still hung. He knew that, didn't he? Clem'd use it to terrify people to death and get what he and his family wanted. But that was a reassuring thought, because so far what he'd done was be vile on the computer and desecrate the dead, all of which could be done without any devil's help.

Chances were, then, that he was lying. And if he was lying, then he had to have some other way of up and disappearing like he'd vanished into thin air.

Ruan hesitated. He could think of one. The prehistoric people who'd put up Dickie and the Five Fingers had obviously loved Jennifer's land as much as Jennifer did, because those weren't the only things they'd built. Couple of hundred yards away from Dickie was the long lying stone that was the lintel of a tomb. A fogou they were called, apparently. Clem could have got there, squirmed inside, be hiding, hoping everyone would scatter to look for him, and he'd be able to sneak out and up to his car then.

Everything had happened so fast, Jennifer and Sam were still on their knees next to Tiger's body, Sam holding the wound shut, Jennifer ripping at the inside of her coat. They were trying to save the dog's life, and Ruan couldn't interrupt that.

He picked up a hand-sized stone and walked over the brow of the small hill he stood on, to where the chamber tomb had been sunk into the ground on the other side. It didn't look like much. From above it was just a long, grey stone splotched with yellow lichen, lying embedded in the grass, but when he circled round and down, two more stones came into view—these two standing upright, supporting the third. Between the stones, a foot-tall rectangle of darkness was all that could be seen of the short passageway into the hill and the corbelled room beyond it.

Ruan crouched outside, tried to peer in. "You can't hide in here, Clem Lusmoore. I know where you are. Come on out to me, or I'll send Jennifer in with her gun."

No response. His voice echoed from the small stone room with a whispery hiss that made him shiver. He'd played around by these ruins often enough as a child. He'd never yet heard them sound like that.

"Don't make me come in there," he tried again, with the shakes coming back and his head splitting. Being the hero was not all it was cracked up to be.

Again, he heard a noise out of the ground that he had never heard before. A faint rustling, like a far-off hollow sigh. It made his skin crawl. He didn't—really didn't—want to go in.

At least Clem had left him his phone. He held it tight as he switched on its flashlight app and sent the bright beam under the earth. It picked up sharp edges of neatly fitted stone, soil in the cracks. Soil underfoot on the floor of the chamber and brutally cut slabs of stone for the sides and roof.

Clem was not inside, but the floor was strange. It had never been lumpy like that. Never been rucked up in that strange triangular mound. He raised his torch higher for a better look and saw a line of utter black beneath the mound, a darkness that his light couldn't touch.

So now he had to put his shoulders through the narrow gap of death's door and squirm the rest of him inside to follow. Five halting doubled-up paces and then he was through, into the burial chamber. It had always been a calm little ovoid with a smooth floor, but now he could see that beneath a section of that apparently beaten earth floor there had been a canvas laid over a trapdoor.

Now the canvas had been rolled back with the earth inside it, like a chewy and tasteless Swiss roll. The trap door had opened, but had not been closed again and beneath it . . . Ruan peered straight down, seeing a long drop, a ladder set into the side of the rock. The torch's light wouldn't penetrate to the bottom of the shaft, but out of it came the sound that had frightened him—the sound like that of cold water dragons breathing in their sleep. It was the distant sea heard through the maze of smugglers' tunnels beneath the whole headland.

Clem had run for home. He thought he was safe. But Ruan wasn't having that. Let the bastard know what it was like to be the prey, for once. He certainly wasn't turning back now.

Switching his phone off to conserve the battery, Ruan swung his feet into utter darkness, and hyperventilating only a little, he pursued.

CHAPTER TWENTY-FOUR

Eighty-one steps on the ladder down from the fogou. The ladder was modern—steel and rubber treads that had barely had time to discolour or rust—but the shaft looked like it had been chipped out of the bedrock with a miner's pick and hammer two hundred years ago. It made Ruan mad angry to think that he had played in the hollow and this had been under his feet all along. Why hadn't he spotted it? But then why should he have thought to try peeling back the earth to see if there was anything beneath it?

Finding this here was like a trespass on his childhood. This was Gwynn land for Gwynn kids. It wasn't fair that the whole thing should have been undermined all along by someone else.

The resentment added to his anger, helped him straighten up when he reached the passage beneath and square his shoulders. It was about time someone stood up to these people, and right now he felt like he wanted to be the one that did.

Only a glimmering of twilight made it through the tomb entrance, into the chamber and down into the passages. He peered as hard as he could into the gloom, hoping to catch the tail end of Clem's light, if he had one, but they all seemed equally black.

Switching his phone back on, he swept the damp darkness with his torch. Three ways met here: one going out towards the mainland; one down, probably towards Constantine Bay. He took a moment to stand with his head cocked, trying to hear Clem's retreating footsteps, but only the rumour of the sea came back.

Guessing that Clem was headed for his computer, Ruan took the third passage, which seemed to go east, towards the warehouses beneath the Angel.

About five hundred yards down the passage, he came out into another junction. He'd known there were caves, of course—they were part of local folklore—but a network of tunnels down in the dark beneath the everyday lives most of the people of Porthkennack lived? That was new, and it creeped him out, right enough. From now on he was always going to be wondering what was crawling by under his feet.

He chose the east passage again, opening his notepad on the phone and keeping a record of his turns so that he could find his way back. Then he went on, with the light held before him like a golden shield, trying to go as quietly and as quickly as possible in the hope of catching up with Clem.

Grey stone disappeared into the dark behind him, and grey stone disappeared into the dark in front. The temperature was faintly warmer than it had been outside, and he had expected still air, so when it went whispering past his ear, laced with cold dew, he shuddered.

Another turn, and a growing feeling that he was already a ghost, that he would be walking under the earth here forever along with all the dead pirates and the smugglers and the foolish excisemen who'd tried to do something like this before him.

Ruan's adrenaline wore off and left the pain in his bruised head to flower into a throbbing universe. This, too, made it hard to think, but one certain thought forced its way in anyway: what was he *doing*?

He passed another junction—steps to the left, a rising, twisting narrow passage to the right, everything still obviously dug out by hand. What *was* he doing? The Lusmoores'd had hundreds of years down here to dig out their kingdom. Might have a city for all he knew, and he was just going to walk into their domain and demand justice?

The footing was still good, but already it was overlaid in his mind with the slippery rocks he'd slid on above black pools full of boulders as sharp as blades. *Watch where you're stepping, mate. Could fall in a lake down here and no one would ever know where you'd gone.*

The thought brought him to a stop at last. Sam and Jennifer *didn't* know where he'd gone. They'd look up from bandaging poor Tiger, and they'd wonder what the hell had happened. *Shit!* It would be as though Clem had disappeared him somehow. Would they think to look in the fogou?

Worse than that, was he actually following Clem at all? There were so many passages—what if Clem had doubled back, climbed out of the fogou, leaving Ruan to wander round like the ancient mariner in search of an illusion. What if Clem had closed the trap door and smoothed the soil down over it? And then, while Sam and Jennifer were taking Tiger to the house, Clem had walked, blithe as you please back to his car and driven away?

Ruan wasn't some kung-fu hero anyway. What did he think he could do, down here alone?

Cold inside and out, he shivered like he'd had his head doused in icy water. See? This was why he needed Sam. This was why he needed someone who knew better than to go running full tilt into every goddamn thing life offered.

One of these days your enthusiasm might get you killed, Ruan. This might actually be that day.

Okay. No need to panic. He took a deep breath to force down the feeling of failure and shame, then turned around. This was fine. He'd almost got himself in trouble, but he'd drawn back in time. Instead of running his nose into a trap, he would retrace his steps and talk to Auntie Jennifer. Jennifer would talk to the rest of the clan. Nan or Gramps could talk to the other families, and the whole native population, the families that had been here since the rocks, could force the Lusmoores to do something about Clem or face the consequences.

Then Ruan could go back to planning tattoos and persuading Sam to stay—to stay and give their joint venture a go. To stay because Ruan didn't want him to leave.

That was a much better plan. With a lighter heart, he flicked his phone screen over to the notepad. His torch app flickered and dimmed, and he remembered like a clutch around the throat that he hadn't remembered to charge the phone last night.

No. Don't!

Seized by the knowledge that it was all about to go horribly wrong, Ruan launched himself into a run. Left at the next turn. He took five steps towards it and the light went out, the low-battery bar red across the top of the screen. One minute of battery life left.

"No! I should have ten minutes. I should have ten minutes, you piece of shit!"

With a smug little whirring grind, the phone powered itself off.

It seemed like forever—he stopped existing, only a ragged panting to tell him that he was still around. His brain seemed to have powered off with the light, and a dread like the heaviness of the earth above him pulled in the chokehold around his throat.

It was his headache that brought him back at first—he became aware of it like a grey pulsing where his eyes should be, and with it came thirst and that panicked breathing. With these things as a guide, he reassembled himself. Wiggling his toes in his boots, clenching and unclenching his fists, he found the limits of his body that he could no longer see. He tucked the useless phone into his pocket by instinct, and the touch was a comfort, so he followed it by reaching both hands up to cover his face, to feel his hair, bouncy and long against his palm.

There he was, look. He hadn't been annihilated at all, it was just dark. He could handle this. He remembered the turnings, didn't he? He could find his way back by memory and touch. If it took a little longer, that wouldn't kill him.

Hand stretched out, he moved sideways until he met a wall. Pretty sure he was still facing the direction he'd been going, he started walking again, hand sliding gently over the rough, wet stone. Now he couldn't see, the smell started to get to him: wet earth, cold and wormy and grave-like. He pulled his scarf up over his nose, closed his eyes to avoid the madness of not being able to see with them open, and walked slowly on.

That wasn't so bad, for a time. But after a long while he thought, *Didn't I just pass a junction? There should have been a junction with stairs on one side. I should have come to that by now.* And even in the cold a wave of sticky, sickly heat rose to the root of his hair and made his bruised forehead squeal.

Maybe the junction had been on the other side of the corridor? He didn't think that was so, because there'd been openings on both sides, but maybe he wasn't remembering it right? Maybe he'd not walked as far as he'd thought, and that junction was still to come?

Or it might be that in trying to get to the corridor walls, he'd got turned around and he was still heading east, away from the exit, down towards the warehouses under the Angel.

His heartbeat thundered in his ears—he could hear the blood rushing there, mingling with the ever-present and useless whisper of the sea. Torn between punching the wall and bursting into tears, he dropped down instead and wrapped his hand around his now healed sun-disc tattoo.

He didn't know why it helped, but it did. It did so. Even though it was no longer any warmer than the rest of his ankle, it felt like there was a spot of light there, just a single spot of light, like a candle in the palm of his hand, and it didn't let him see, but he felt like it lit the dark regardless.

If he went back, he could spend hours going back and forward looking for this junction and by the time he found it he'd have forgotten which way to go next. He'd go on. Either he'd reach the exit onto Jennifer's land, or he'd reach another, or he'd reach the warehouses, and he had some chance of remembering the path out from there. That's what he'd do. He wasn't lost yet.

He had pictures of Sam in his mind as he went on. Sam with the golden sunset in his hair and the water glittering all over him silver-gilt. Sam in the warmth of Jennifer's kitchen telling him they'd make it out of this. Telling him Ruan just had to hold on to the light and he'd make it through.

He should have stuck with Sam. *I will do next time*, he told whoever might be listening in the darkness. *Please. If you give me the chance, I'll do better next time. I thought it was my job to make him strong, but I forgot it was his to do likewise for me.*

In this state of surrender, he walked on. It felt like at least a mile, and there were no more junctions. He fought off despair two or three times, definitely, officially lost, and then . . .

A boom. A booming rumble from ahead of him. He snapped his eyes open and caught the edge, the very edge of the shape of a stone ahead of him. It took his dazed brain a moment to realize that was light. There was light spilling down the passage ahead of him. His hands were a dull blur when he raised them, but he could see that blur right there.

Like a man thirsty after weeks in the desert, he picked up his pace, almost running towards the light, and then, when he could see enough to make it safe, *actually* running, eager—no, desperate—to get the fuck out of here, to get back into the day.

That wasn't daylight, mind. Underneath his instinctive rush, his mind was finally back at work. 'Cause that was electric light, certain sure. And now he could see the door that stood ajar at the end of the passage—a sea door like something out of a submarine, the back of it industrial cream blotched with crawling stains of rust.

Whatever had made the booming sound in that room beyond could have been Clem. If he'd not been that far behind the man despite it all, he could still be coming out of the wall just behind Clem.

Ruan paused on the threshold, hand on the door. Well, so. He could deal with Clem. He'd dealt with him before. And the only way out was through. Through or back into the pressing claustrophobia of the dark. That was no choice at all. He opened the door, quiet-like, hoping to sneak out unseen and hide himself somewhere, behind a packing crate or a stalagmite, whatever he was offered.

But the first thing he saw in the room was the insultingly poor artwork tattooed into the back of Martin Lusmoore's hand, while the man tapped the end of a crowbar meaningfully into his other palm. Harry, behind him, had a bike chain wrapped around one fist. Behind both of them—hiding behind them—Clem gave Ruan a shit-eating grin. Of course. He'd had time to prepare for this. He'd been waiting.

"You'd better come all the way in, boy," Martin growled. "'Cause it won't go well for you if you make us chase you."

CHAPTER
TWENTY-FIVE

Sam fought with his clenching breath as his slippery fingers tried to both hold together the edges of Tiger's wound and press down enough to stop the blood. At first, Tiger had tried to bite him, tried to surge up to his feet and run away from Sam's determined grip, and that had been terrible: trying to keep him down, to push the teeth away, not sure at that point whether their attacker would be coming back with some other weapon.

But Jennifer had thumped down to Sam's side with a grunt, throwing her shotgun aside. "That'll see him off," she said as she leaned in to examine the wound. "Oh, Tiger, my old lad, what has he done to you?"

She'd nodded to Sam, which he took to mean, *Keep doing what you're doing*, and taking off her jacket, had extricated a pocket knife and started to cut the lining into strips.

Sam hadn't dared look away from the dog, but he'd assumed she meant she had either shot the chainsaw—which would explain why he didn't hear it any more—or she'd shot the miscreant himself. With the blood seeping thickly between his fingers, he didn't care which.

There was no bite left in the dog by the time Sam accepted the pad of lining material and pressed that on instead. Tiger's head had drooped to the ground, but he was still whimpering in high heartbreaking notes with his lips pulled back from his teeth and his paws jerking. Sam helped raise him up so Jennifer could wind the long spiral bandage she had made around the dog, over the top of the pad to hold it tight.

"We've got to get him to the vet," she hissed, white-eyed, urgent. "Right away. I don't know how long he's going to last like this. We'll put him on my coat and carry him between us."

But with his hands free and the bandage in place, Sam had time to look up. It was strange that Ruan of all people had not rushed back from driving their assailant off and thrown himself to his knees and done anything, everything he could think of to help, asked for or not. Where was he?

Maybe he'd been able to see that what they'd needed was space to manoeuvre? Maybe he was standing on the edge of the hollow, with his arms across his chest, broody and wind-blown and a tiny bit melodramatic.

But when Sam scoured the landscape for a sight of him, this hopeful fantasy—so unlike his normal glass-empty-and-smashed view of the world—was revealed at once for the nonsense it was. The sun had risen as they worked and he could see from one side of the peninsula to the other, over its green humped back from sea to sea. Ruan was not there.

Horror speared through Sam like the tines of a garden fork. Was Ruan lying in a ditch, dead, concealed by tussocky grass? No. Surely he was just . . .

Hiding somewhere?

That made no sense. So where was he? Oh God, had that cruel young man somehow kidnapped him, thinking to move from intimidation to murder? What was Ruan suffering right now?

"Ruan!" he screamed, scarcely aware that it was his voice, though it tore out of his throat like he had torn out his heart. "Ruan!"

No answer. Up in the copse, a robin broke into inappropriate song, and on the downs they could hear the ever-present squabbling of seagulls. Traffic on the distant main road was a quiet rush and rumble. But nothing from Ruan, not a footfall or a word.

Sam threw himself to his feet and staggered through a three-hundred-and-sixty-degree turn, trying to make himself believe he would see something this time. Ruan would be there this time. He was panicking for nothing, like he always did. It would turn out to be false, like it always did. Wouldn't it? "Where *is* he?"

Jennifer's small hand caught his elbow and squeezed so hard that the pain interrupted his freak out like a slap to the face. "I don't know," she growled, her face as grey as her hair. "But we gotta get Tiger back to the house. Help me pick him up."

Sam shook his head desperately. There was too much—too much urgency, too many vital things that he should be doing but couldn't do all at once. Trying to force his mind to work was like trying to contain a cloud of panicking bats between both hands. Everything was scrabbling, biting, trying to burst apart and fly out.

He lurched into the chilly, dry back of the standing stone and fell to his knees there, pressing his cheek to the stone. Letting everything else fall away except for the texture against his skin, he froze his spiralling thoughts in the cold. One thing. What one thing should he do now?

Forcing himself to think slowly, he acknowledged that he couldn't help Ruan until he knew what had happened to him, knew where he was, and he didn't know those things. But he *could* help Tiger. So with his heart hollow and his tendons screaming, he peeled himself shakily away from the stone and helped roll the dog onto Jennifer's spread-out jacket. Then he took the shoulders as she took the hem, and heaved. Between them, the weight was light, and the stretcher of the coat made it easier to carry the dog smoothly while they jogged for the farmhouse.

"Alana! Alana!" Jennifer shouted as they ran through the boot room minutes later.

The door opened from the barn, and Alana stormed in in wellies and tweeds, an empty dog food bowl in one hand. The colour had come back to her face, and she was Amazonian, ready to take on the world again, her long, ash-coloured plait swinging over her shoulder. She took one look at Tiger and ran to grab keys from the hall. "I'm going to save asking what's happened until later. Put him in the Land Rover. I'll take him straight to the vet's."

Another time, Sam might have been able to appreciate such a pair of formidable battleaxes. Right now he just wanted them to go faster so he could get back to worrying about Ruan.

Quickly, but gently, he set Tiger down in the back of Alana's Landy and helped Jennifer pad the dog with sofa cushions so he wouldn't slide around when she roared around the corners. He closed the back door, watched Alana throw herself in the driving seat and accelerate off, clods of mud flying from the wheels.

In the shaken silence that followed, every part of Sam said, *Ruan*. Every cell in his body said, *Ruan*, and only willpower kept them from imploding altogether at the fear that he might not see him again. This was a hell of a time to discover that he couldn't live without the man. But not even his powerful rational intellect could tell him that option was definitely off the cards.

"Where would Ruan have gone?" He turned back to where Jennifer stood, bereft and bloodstained in front of the house. "How could he have disappeared?"

Visibly—her shoulders rising and then falling with a great, restraining breath—she put down her worry for Tiger and picked up the next concern. "Come on," she said. "I'll introduce you to Washcloth."

The sentence made no sense, and Sam had no patience for chasing it down until it did. He followed her around the outside of the house, through the sheep pens into the barn. There, in a breeze-block kennel, an ancient white-muzzled bloodhound was dozing on a pile of straw. It perked up when Jennifer rattled its gate, and creaked to its feet, stiffly walking out to nose at her hand.

"This is Washcloth—don't ask. My dad's, from when he rode to hounds. And don't look at me like that. Some dogs won't take to the house. She likes a pen—it's what she's used to."

She'd obviously interpreted his nonplussed gaze as a rebuke, but the truth was he was far too busy holding his panic to have even been listening. "What . . .?"

"She's a bloodhound, so? I happened to see you're wearing Ruan's scarf. You let her sniff that to remind her, and she'll find him for us, certain sure."

Stop it! Sam thought at himself, fighting back another wave of terror. His body was urging him to scream, to pace back and forth, clutch his hair, until he exhausted himself enough to fall down. If he kept breathing this hard, he might black out, have to be sent to the hospital. *And that's not going to do him any good. There's a plan. Jennifer has a plan. So keep it together and follow the plan. Don't . . .*

His body was shaking, his fingertips numb, his lips stinging. A shrill whining noise in his head kept dopplering in and out like an ill-tuned radio station, and he needed to throw up, to curl forward over the pain in his chest and rock in the dark until everything went away. He wasn't sure what he looked like, but it must have been bad, because Jennifer gave a not-entirely-unsympathetic snort and unwound his scarf for him.

She unlatched the gate of the pen and let the bloodhound out. Washcloth buried her nose in Jennifer's cupped hands. "All right there, girl?" she said, slipping her a dog treat with one hand while she clipped a lead onto her collar with the other. "Let's just find Ruan, shall we?"

She wadded up the scarf and held it out. Washcloth plunged her nose into the centre of it and snuffled eagerly, tail swishing. "That's it, lass, find Ruan. Can you find him?"

Washcloth loped slowly to the door of the barn, nose now questing over the ground. She didn't resist being gently towed towards the hills. In fact, after the first five minutes, her gait loosened, her tail rose, and it looked like she was enjoying herself. Sam forgave her for it only when they reached the stone and she gave a yip and a bay of discovery and began tugging on Jennifer's leash.

His stomach churning, Sam noticed with a shock that the body still hung on the stone, even more grotesque and pitiable in the light of day. Sam was glad to put it behind him and follow the dog up to within view of the road. Maybe Ruan had been locked up in the back seat of that parked car? Knocked out but fine? That wouldn't be so bad.

But Washcloth circled them round and down the side of a small hill, and there was a stone opening in the grass, like something Irish, Elvish, like the entrance to another world.

The dog went in, tail wagging, Jennifer crawling after her without a sign of fear.

Sam, when he thought about it, was not afraid of prehistoric monuments. In fact, the prospect calmed him. He followed, found the empty chamber and a shaft straight down.

"I might have known. I might have known." Jennifer was shaking her head, her hands half covering her mouth. "Oh the bastards, this has gone too far."

A cold air came up from the hole in the earth as Sam leaned over to look in. These were the famous Lusmoore caves, were they?

And Ruan had revisited them for some reason, despite his fright. "Ruan's in there?"

"Seems that way." Jennifer scrubbed her hand through her silver hair. "At any rate the dog thinks so. I need to get the clans together. This calls for a delegation."

"Do you suppose they're . . . holding him captive, somehow? Against his will, I mean?"

She creaked a weary smile as if she'd seen this all before, too many times. "If they've found him poking about down there? They'll probably have put him somewhere while they try to decide what to do with him. I don't think they'd hurt him; he's a Gwynn. But there'll need to be some bargaining before they'll let him go."

Sam peered down into the darkness again. It was only stone and peace, the quiet of closed eyes to him, but what must Ruan be going through down there, hunted or imprisoned? "How long will that take?"

"I can't see everyone agreeing to do anything before tomorrow. And there's the police still to phone, and that poor girl to put back to rest. Tomorrow, maybe the day after." She took another glance at his face and must have made a better guess at the dread and the agony in his heart. "He'll be fucking scared, and they might lay a hand on him, I won't deny it. But once they know the families know he's in Lusmoore hands, there'll be no real harm."

"What if they're harming him already?" Sam insisted, unable to let it go. His body was still stammering around him, neurons misfiring, nerves so wound up they were shaking him apart, but it was all drowned out by the bright white light of his fear for Ruan. "What if—right now—they aren't aware that anyone knows where he is? What if they think he can just disappear and no one will ever know? Can you tell me for sure they wouldn't make the decision to kill him *before* you could get your clans involved?"

Washcloth was whining on the edge of the shaft, pawing the turned earth there, eager to go on with the chase. Jennifer dropped a soothing hand onto her head, though it seemed the comfort was for her rather than the dog—she was the only one who looked defeated. Her shoulders slumped. "I suppose I can't. Not fully."

Then it wasn't a choice, was it? Sam couldn't imagine surviving the stress of not knowing if Ruan would be okay for a whole day or more. His heart would give out. He had to move, had to act, or he would never be able to live with himself again.

"Then let me carry the dog down to guide me, and I'll go after him."

CHAPTER TWENTY-SIX

It wasn't so bad in the caves, especially if Sam didn't think about what he was doing. He fell back on the mindfulness his last therapist had insisted would cure everything, and simply concentrated on the ghost sensations of vision in pitch-blackness, where white shapes that were his own synapses firing floated in front of his staring eyes. With a hand on the wall, he could walk slowly but surely behind Washcloth's elderly pace, feeling for the roughness of the path with his shoes, not needing light.

There was something rather soothing about the quiet, and the way the dog's waving tail would tap his shin if he got too close. *"You keep her safe,"* Jennifer had insisted, almost angrily. *"I wouldn't let her go but for Ruan. So you've got to promise to bring her back unharmed, you hear? Look after her."*

Sam had promised, obviously, but at the moment Washcloth was looking after him. Her panting was a metronome, helping him keep his sense of time. A pattern emerged in the syncopation of their footsteps with their breathing, and he found its mathematical variations as calming as the sound of water moving over the stones in the small brook outside his van.

The warmth in his heart when he thought of Foxglove Copse suggested that he had formed an emotional attachment to the place, put down roots. And it was true that he would like to see the copse in springtime, when there would be white and pink flowers, and all the new twigs would glow with rusty Day-Glo colours. How nice it would be to live there in the summer, out in the bender tent, watching the stars through the leaves at night, Ruan in his arms.

Washcloth stopped and snuffled. He could feel her casting about by the tiny wriggles of the leash in his hand and then she was tugging forward again and once more he plodded behind with his fingertips being grated off by the walls and a comforting illusion that this was it now—that he was doomed to walk here like this forever. That there was, and never had been, anything else in the world but this darkness.

That was a lie, because there had been Ruan. Ruan, who teetered delightfully on the cusp between boy and man. Who had a man's body but a child's enthusiasm, trust . . . No, he wasn't thinking about how easily a child's trust could be betrayed. Better to think about the endearing, doglike affectionate nature of the man. Ruan didn't seem to have a mean bone in his body, perhaps the only person in Sam's life who had ever made him feel safe enough to relax.

Fuck you all! Don't hurt him. Don't take him away!

The cry of pain slipped through his defences, all-consuming for a moment, so powerful he thought it should have rattled the earth above his head. But it passed and changed nothing, and he walked onward, shaking a little harder as he went.

It helped that he still couldn't quite believe this. One thing he had from his middle-class, suburban upbringing was an absolute conviction that everyone on earth appreciated the rule of law. Crime didn't happen to people like him. Organized crime certainly didn't happen in his country, and pirates and smugglers were semilegendary creatures best thought of in association with mermaids and sea serpents. He was not—absolutely not—walking into the lair of a pirate queen. The very idea was ridiculous.

He was not quite deluded enough to believe that made everything all right, but it helped.

Simply, then, trying not to think about a lot of things, Sam walked on, following Washcloth the bloodhound through two more junctions and then down a long straight featureless passage that went on forever.

It went on forever, and then it suddenly stopped with a closed door. Thin slivers of light spilled through around the edges of the rectangle, letting him see enough of the metal handle to reach out and grasp it.

Terror boiled into him with the touch. Out here in the dark, just him and the dog, everything was okay. Nothing to be scared of in rocks, quiet, or the sibilance of the sea. But through this door?

There would be people. Hostile people. There would be people who might . . . He didn't have the imagination to worry about being hit, but they might shout. They would laugh at him, belittle, mock him.

He would go to pieces. He would not be able to speak because his teeth were chattering too hard, and his voice would seize in his throat. They'd think it was because he was a coward—and he *was*. He *was* a coward if he couldn't do this for Ruan. Just do an easy thing like pushing the door handle down and swinging the door open. Stepping through into the light.

Other people could do things like that but he . . . he'd probably trip over his own feet and fall, smack his head on something and knock himself out—get flung into the sea next to Ruan, accomplishing nothing. Or maybe they'd hurt Ruan and make him watch. Or they'd hurt *him* and Ruan would be angry that he'd come, because he'd made everything worse.

He was not . . . not good at this. What the hell had possessed him to think that he ought to have tried?

For a despicable moment, he actually took his hand off the lever and stepped back, turned a little to see the light fade out on the edges of the tunnel through which he had come.

He couldn't do this. But nor could he give up and walk away. He had run out of options. He couldn't do anything at all.

Washcloth scraped at the base of the door, whining. "Shh," he whispered to her even as she returned to lick his fingers. "Don't let them hear you."

Oh, but that was familiar, wasn't it? He'd had a built-in wardrobe in his room where he had grown up—the only part of the house he remembered fondly. This was like crouching in there, in the dark, while Mum and Dad and Tabitha had been screaming at each other downstairs. Wondering if they'd murder Tabby or if she would make a pact with them and they'd all come up and murder him.

But he couldn't keep hiding like this. He'd escaped from them— he'd been clever enough and smart enough and resilient enough to get out of that house. That must mean he could do something here too. He was not helpless. Not yet, at least. And if he failed now, it would not be because he'd been too afraid to try. For himself, he'd stay in the dark, but for Ruan?

The handle and the hinges of the door squealed with rust as he turned the latch and pushed the door open, revealing a blessedly lit and empty room beyond.

He took three steps down into what could have been a wine cellar. Packing crates from ships had been stacked around the walls. Two desks at the focus of a spider's web of cabling contained two PCs, one powered down and one running, with an ancient screen saver drawing multicoloured pipes over its screen.

Washcloth was tugging him towards the further door, but he couldn't pass that computer without leaning over to roll the mouse across its pad. The screensaver flicked off, and there it was—one of the troll's Twitter accounts, "innocently" displaying a list of tweets from the girls Sam knew and from others.

So he was getting somewhere. That thought bolstered him as he followed the dog quietly across the room. The further door was also closed, but voices came indistinctly from beneath it and scraped up Sam's spine like bony fish teeth.

Could he turn back even now?

No, he couldn't. Therefore he had to go on.

He pushed the door open and walked through, and there was the troll, his asymmetric hair long on one side, undercut on the other, his cheeks purple with acne. For a moment, Sam thought the shaved lines of the triskele in the stubble was a swastika, silver on his scalp. Then, as he looked properly, he realized that the boy was younger than him. Younger than Ruan. The same age as the girls who had come to Sam for his help. The same age as Linda.

Abruptly, he was less frightened and more infuriated. It didn't matter that the troll wasn't alone—he had two friends with him— what mattered was the truth, the rightness of the universe, the things that Sam could and could not put up with.

"Where's Ruan?" he said, loud and authoritative, with a calm that surprised him.

"Who the fuck's this then?" the troll's blond compatriot slapped him hard on the shoulder as if he blamed everything on the boy. The second strode over to Sam and grabbed his wrist, twisting it up behind him in a fluid, practised hold.

"I don't know. He's that faggot that was with him," the troll muttered, rubbing his shoulder and staring at the floor.

"My name's Sam Atkins." Sam almost smiled at this onslaught of sudden bravery, but he didn't know how long it would last, so he wasted no time in getting his message out, while he could still speak. Already, despite his rush of glory, he could feel the shake starting to work its way up through his calves, trying to rise into his belly and his heart.

"I came to tell you that you can't hurt Ruan. His people know you're behind the bullying and the witchcraft. You were caught on camera stringing up that poor girl on Jennifer's land. And if Ruan and I don't come back safely, the Gwynns want you to know that they're going to hand the whole matter over to the police. You can get away with scare tactics, but you can't get away with murder."

The blond guy and the man restraining Sam exchanged a glance. The grip on Sam's arm was immovable but not cruel, and he was unreasonably reassured by the man's resemblance to Captain Birdseye—half expected him to break out a smile and a fish-finger sandwich.

"What makes you think we got anything to do with Ruan Gwynn at all?" the Captain asked, sounding disgruntled.

"The dog was tracking him," Sam panted, as Blondy crouched down beside Washcloth and offered her his hand. She considered it a moment and then licked from his fingertips into his palm. A fine bloodhound but clearly a poor judge of character.

"Well you're a right'un ent you?" Blondy told her happily. He rubbed behind her ears, and the dog half closed her eyes and grinned at him, her tongue lolling out and one long ear brushing the tip of his boot.

"You should knock him on the head and toss him in one of the pools," the troll said, watching this evidence of humanity with a surly eye. "Who's going to know?"

But his voice had lost the declaiming, theatrical ring it had held when he yelled at Ruan by the stone. He sounded like a teenager now—whiny, powerless, hard done by.

"You shut up, you." Captain Birdseye eased the pressure on Sam's shoulder and glowered at the boy. "What're you up to anyway, drawing all these people down the tunnels? I don't mind punching a guy who's been giving you grief, but we're not your fucking private army, boy."

"I'm just doing what I was—"

"Shut. Up."

For a brief bare moment, Sam felt sorry for the troll. It must be hard, growing up as a boy with crime lords as your role models, wanting to exceed—wanting to be bigger and meaner and scarier so you could get some respect. But the feeling didn't last long.

"Where is Ruan?" he said again.

"Ooh, you're a lovely girl. You're a right old lady."

Sam thought Blondy had ignored him completely, until the man craned sideways over the dog's head and caught the Captain's eye, half shamefaced, half resigned. "We can't hurt the dog, Marty. Maybe we'd better just shove 'em both in the locker and let Grandma decide what to do."

So a moment later, Sam was propelled to the end of the further corridor and pushed through a metal door. They looked like they were going to coax Washcloth through more gently, but she took a sniff of the air and bolted in, baying. Sam's heart gave an answering peal at the sound, as Ruan took advantage of the last of the light as the door swung shut, hurled himself at Sam, and wrapped himself round like an octopus, clinging, clinging tight.

"Oh fuck! Oh fuck, Sam!" Ruan muttered, his face in Sam's neck, his voice thick and shaking, his cheeks wet against Sam's skin.

Sam held on just as tightly, his own fear still subsumed by Ruan, by the startled revelation that when Ruan was in his arms, it was hard to be desperately anxious about anything. "Shhh," he whispered, dropping a kiss on Ruan's eyebrow and letting the man's tears soak into his shirt. "It's okay. I've got you."

Right now, that was enough.

CHAPTER
TWENTY-SEVEN

Things had gone badly for Ruan. Harry had punched him, right in the mouth, with that chain wrapped round his knuckles, and Ruan's front teeth had felt as wobbly as his knees had after, as they hauled him shocked and limp through the packed warehouse and out to a little cell on the other side. They'd thrown him in and shut the door. Another one of those ship-board doors, metal, rubber round the outside, shutting flush into the stone, letting no breath of air or touch of light through.

He hadn't known he was afraid of the dark neither. Not before all of this. Down at home there was always light, out on the seafront, mast lights nodding on the anchored trawlers, streetlights outside his window. At uni, there'd been a nightclub on the other side of the road from their shared house, with a neon-yellow champagne glass outside that turned into a red, reclining girl in a perpetual flick, flick, flick of moving colour.

He'd never been before in a place where you could open your eyes and see a hole, like the whole world had been shut off. Not before this. Not like this.

Why'd Ruan ever thought he was a hero? Why'd he let himself imagine real life ever worked out like it did in the films? He raised a hand to his face, and the fingertips pattered like rain against his bruises because they were trembling so much. The salt on his skin burned his cut lip as he pressed the bruise, morbidly unable to stop touching its swollen tightness. He thought he'd got all the grease off, but every time he felt it, his hand came away slick.

First off, he'd staggered round the walls, tracing them with his outstretched hands, somehow convinced that they'd grown since that brief glimpse he'd had when he was thrown inside. Convinced he'd missed the drop-off where they opened into a void that wanted to suck him right down.

He hadn't touched anything like that—only breeze block and paint. His foot had impacted with something that rolled away with a rattle. When he bent over to feel, it turned out to be a big metal bucket. After that, fearful of ramming into the far wall, he was more cautious with his steps, so when he did get to it, he only nudged his toe against it and, reaching down, felt a long, narrow shelf like somewhere you'd put a coffin.

It smelled like somewhere you'd put a coffin too—that dank, wet-earth smell that filled every breath with the certainty of being buried alive.

Ruan had curled up on the bench where he could wedge himself into a corner that pressed on both shoulders, so the only immensity was above and in front of him. If anything, his shaking had gotten worse, the clicking of his teeth sounding like something out there, like the clicking of bone centipedes beyond where the edges of his tactile universe disappeared into the dark.

Was it his panting breath he heard, or was it someone else's? He wouldn't know—not if they were soft footed. If they came quietly, he wouldn't know until they touched him, cold and slimy and wet, like everything down here. God, how he'd scream.

He had felt it rising up in him already, the need to yell and yell as though he could punch some red warmth out of himself and fill the dark with it. When he felt for the sun on his ankle, it gave him no comfort. Stood to reason, didn't it? Down here, the sun couldn't come. Down here, it was night all day long.

Touching his lip made it bleed again, the taste warm and metallic on his tongue. There'd been real malice behind the blow that'd maybe hurt more than the punch itself. No softness, no possibility of relenting. Exactly what he'd been afraid of when he'd been down here last. Time was proving he'd been right to be scared. He'd been wrong to think he could take this on alone. Wrong to think he was brave enough or smart enough to make a difference.

What would his mam and da do if he never came home? The grating, gasping noise of his breath choked off into a sob. What would

Tegan do, feeling like it was her fault, never able to ask for help again in case the same thing happened to someone else? And the rest of his family, his uncles and aunts and cousins? What would they do? Before he knew it, he was crying wrenching tears and wiping his streaming nose against his jeans where he rested his head on his knees.

What would Sam do without him? Would he remember to eat? Would he just go on somewhere else, shut up in that solitary-confinement van of his? Would Jennifer hustle him on to somewhere no one knew him, where he'd be, once more, the convenient outsider on whom the local shit could be pinned? Somehow the void of that idea was the coldest and darkest of all.

It wasn't right. It wasn't fair! But he couldn't find it in him to do more than cry about it, not while it meant crossing all that empty dark to bang on the door and beg to be let out.

Sound came to him suddenly, hitting him like another punch. He bolted upright. What was that? A metallic jangle. Keys!

Bright as a floating ember, a keyhole appeared—someone outside must have drawn back a cover. It was still visible when the key was put in and turned. The door separated from the wall in a thermonuclear blaze of radiance that knocked him back, eyes streaming. But there was gold in it.

Squinting, he tried to focus—gold like summer, bright and warm and easy. Gold like . . . Oh!

Joy came bounding up from inside him and shook him like a great dog shaking a rabbit. That gold was Sam's hair. It couldn't be. It couldn't be—the man was delicate, fragile, he wouldn't have dared *come after Ruan*. He wouldn't have, couldn't have pushed through eviscerating terror and honed helplessness just because Ruan needed him. Would he?

But Ruan's imagination would never have conjured Sam up with Washcloth by his side, Jennifer's arthritic old bloodhound with her tail up high and her snout raised in a bay of triumph because she was such a good girl and she knew it. Ruan's imagination would have gone for something more epic and three thousand percent less welcome.

"Oh fuck! Oh fuck, Sam!" he gasped, lurching to his feet and flinging himself at the man, drinking him in while there was light to do so, huddling as close as he could get when it was quenched again.

"Shhh," Sam soothed. "It's okay. I've got you."

Sam had come to rescue him, and though nothing else had changed, he had succeeded. Ruan *felt* rescued. It was amazing.

"I need to sit down," he managed when he had got his ribs closed up again from where that explosion of happiness had blown them apart. His breath was slowing, but his knees were shaky, and he was so tired all at once. "Back here, there's a kind of bed."

Like in an ungainly three-legged race, they shuffled over to the bench tangled together. Ruan wedged himself back in the corner, and Sam settled over his outstretched legs, kneeling there. Sam's back was to the dark, but Ruan was now protected by stone and the warmth of Sam's chest. Sam's fingers brushed over his face, wiping away tears, finding his mouth, and then Sam kissed him. Shallow at first, just a soft warmth against him, but coaxing his mouth open with little licks and, as Ruan closed his eyes and relaxed into it, deepening into proper possessiveness and passion. Heat welled from within him and drove away the shivering.

They might have taken it further if Washcloth hadn't been scrabbling and whining to get up too. Ruan was tempted to ignore her for a little while longer, but she was old and stiff and she'd helped Sam find him. He owed her a bit of comfort in return.

"Lift her up will you, poor lass," he said, aware it was nothing close to what he wanted to say.

Sam snorted into the dark. It was a friendlier place with him in it. He climbed off Ruan, and when he climbed back on, it was to lie between Ruan's legs, back resting against Ruan's chest. The dog walked her hard paws over their knees and settled between them, licking Ruan's ankle over the sock.

If anything, everything had honestly got worse, but Ruan couldn't feel that. Sam was in his arms, Washcloth lying content and snoozing over his feet, warming them, and suddenly even the dark was a balm.

"I can't believe you came after me." He tried to put the joy he'd felt into words, but they didn't come out right. "I mean, I know you're brave. I just thought you . . . you didn't like people much. I never thought you'd come for *me*—'cause of that."

"I don't like people, in general." Sam sounded watery now, like it was his turn to cry. "But that makes you unique. You're . . ." he leaned his head against Ruan's cheek, so Ruan could feel the shape of his words as they curled that lovely pink mouth of his, "irreplaceable. I don't think there's another person like you in the world, Ruan."

He laced one hand through Ruan's right hand, drawing Ruan's arm closer around him, clasping his other hand on top. His voice was wild and strained and so sincere. "I couldn't drive away from here and leave you. I couldn't not know what was happening to you. I couldn't *live* . . . I couldn't live without you."

It was the kind of thing you normally said on a date. Something romantic like a boat trip and a picnic or a classy restaurant, and it was nice to hear but hard to believe. But Sam'd gone and proved it, hadn't he? He'd run his neck right into the noose without a qualm, just so they could be together.

By now the room was full of invisible radiance, essential and potent like the dark energy scientists talked about. You could harness this joy up to the national grid and power the world from its aftershocks. Ruan made a small, emasculating squeak and pushed his forehead into Sam's shoulder again.

"Don't go, then," he said again, feeling like although he'd said it before, maybe this time Sam would take him seriously. He'd always meant it, but this time he meant it more. "Stay with me forever and I'll look after you. We'll look after each other, okay?" He lifted his head enough to kiss Sam's shoulder, his throat, his jaw, the edge of his mouth. "You can have all my people. All my family—they'll love you like I do. Because I do. I do love you."

Sam took a shaky breath and said nothing. Maybe because he was speechless. Maybe because they could hear the keys again, and voices wrangling outside their sleepy little private universe, and they both knew this reprieve was coming to an end.

"I *do* love you," Ruan repeated urgently, willing him to believe it before it was too late. "I only hope they let me have the chance to prove it."

Sam drew breath to say something back, only to be silenced by the kettledrum-loud crash of the door against the wall outside, light scouring into the room like a red-hot poker laid across their eyes.

Washcloth leapt to her feet and stood on the bench, hedging her bets by barking and wagging her tail. Ruan looked at Sam and saw him still dazed and dazzled by the light and noise. Like him, Sam was obviously too far away in a place of peace and joy to yet have woken fully to threat.

Martin and Harry Lusmoore seemed to find that insulting. They swaggered in, all swinging arms and smugness. Grabbed Sam and then Ruan, physically hauling them to their feet and pushed them towards the door.

"All right, my lovers," Martin mocked. "Time for you to face the boss."

CHAPTER TWENTY-EIGHT

Grandma Wyn should have seemed out of place in the brutally practical warehouse room they were dragged into. She had obviously been by the hairdresser first, and her hair was rolled into tight curls reminiscent of the queen.

It seemed to be a calculated look. She neatly perched on the better of the two chairs by the computer table, with a white fur jacket folded over the back of the seat, wearing a pink mohair jumper and pearls, and her hands in pink leather gloves to match.

Clem stood at her left-hand side like a royal page, and once Ruan and Sam had been shoved in front of her, the guards strolled over to stand at her shoulders like bodyguards or knights.

In the quiet moment before anything started, her glance flicked over Sam, up and down once before dismissing him. He must have felt it, because he stepped closer to Ruan, close enough that their elbows brushed and Ruan could feel him trembling.

Right. This was a case of dealing with people, and people weren't Sam's strength. The baton of their partnership had firmly been handed over to him.

Even now, that gave him a thrill. Protecting Sam, doing the things he couldn't do? Just the knowledge that he was needed made him more powerful than he'd been alone.

"Ruan Gwynn." Grandma sighed. "What am I going to do with you? I thought we were going to be friends, after I helped you and all."

Ruan took his new confidence and attempted to think his way out of this. "I don't see why we shouldn't be friends, ma'am. I haven't got nothing against you or the Lusmoores in general. It's just Clem there I have a problem with."

"He's a fucking lying fag whatever he says." Clem folded his arms across his chest in a blatant imitation of his cousin Martin.

"There ain't no call for that language, lad." Harry clipped him round the ear with a lazy hand. "Not in front of Grandma. You be quiet now and let the grown-ups talk."

Grandma Wyn rose to her feet, pacing from one corner of the room to its diagonal as if she were formulating difficult thoughts. "I'm glad to hear you don't have a problem with this family," she started, thoughtfully. "Because the Lusmoores have been the lifeblood of this town from before history began. When there was famine in the old days, or Westminster were squeezing us dry for taxes, who d'you think brought in money and food to the whole town?"

"I'm guessing it was your family." Ruan relaxed a little, surprisingly reassured by being lectured like a child.

"It was." Wyn nodded, pacing around the circumference of the room like she couldn't contain herself. "I grew up down here, you know. While the bombs were dropping overhead. It was the safest place in the war, so we had dormitories for all the families, all the kids chasing each other through the passages, playing hide and seek."

Her eyes had warmed, lost in what seemed to be a pleasant memory, though her entourage settled into a sullen silence as though they'd heard it too many times before.

"It was Lusmoore ships that ran the U-boat cordon day by day, bringing in food. Smuggling it, right enough. I don't deny that. But we lost so many sons and brothers and fathers feeding this town. They thought we were heroes then, Ruan Gwynn. They'll think it again. Times change, but we don't. We're true Cornishmen, through and through."

He wasn't sure where she was going with this, but he couldn't go along that far. "You are not," he said, though his voice shook. "Since when are true Cornishmen murderers, bullies, desecraters of corpses? There is no way you can make that okay."

"Don't be dramatic." Wyn waved a gloved hand, but her carefully neutral expression had gained slight frown lines. "Stringing up a few sheep that were going to end up slaughtered anyway? I know you young people get all het up with your 'meat is murder' nonsense, but—"

Clem shifted from one foot to the other, turning his face away from his grand-matron's gaze, and Ruan thought, *Oh.*

"You don't know, do you?" he cut in. "You don't know what's been going on at all."

Wyn stopped her pacing, folded her arms. The gesture brought into high relief the family resemblance between the clan. "Of course I know. I'm only trying to persuade your aunt she's better off selling to me. She's a tough old bird. It's not going to do her any real harm. And she's a bit long in the tooth for farming. I'd give her a fair price for the land . . ."

Behind Ruan's shoulder, Sam huffed out a small laugh. It threw Wyn off her stride and her shrewd eyes narrowed. "Why? What are you talking about if not that?"

"He's a liar, that's what." Clem made a break for the door, but Martin must have been waiting for it, because he got him by the collar almost lazily and dragged him back into place. "I just did what you said. I tried to frighten her off like you said."

Wyn smoothed her coat and her gloves, sat back down, but this time she was looking at Ruan less like a problem to be solved and more like she genuinely wanted to hear what he had to say. As the fear of being flung into a dark pool to break his back on underwater stalagmites ebbed, he groped out with his right hand and took Sam's left, licking his lips and deciding to come out and say it flat.

"You don't know Clem's been harassing young girls on the internet to the point where more'n one of them's killed herself—"

Clem snarled at him, lunging forward in Martin's grip. "That's not true. You can't prove that!"

And he might have felt bad for the lad, except that no, he didn't.

"I can prove it." Sam's voice fell startlingly into the conversation—thin, nervous, obviously pushed out with great effort, but landing like a lightning bolt in the centre of them all.

"You're a fucking outsider, you can fucking shut up." Throughout the interview, Clem had been sounding less and less smug, but at this point it occurred to Ruan that the balance had shifted—that he and Sam were now accusers, not defendants in the court of Grandma Wyn's opinion. A thin psychosomatic pain drew itself out of his bone marrow and disappeared at the thought that perhaps their situation was no longer dire. Perhaps all of this was going to be okay.

"Prove it how?" Wyn asked, finally deigning to look at Sam.

Sam hunched under her gaze, and Ruan squeezed the hand he still held. *You're doing fine.*

"Um . . . Proving the cyberbullying would be complicated and require a specialized—"

"See!" Clem tried to shake himself out of Martin's grasp, ramming his throat into his own collar like a dog on a choke chain. "He can't. He's just making shit up 'cause he's got it in for—"

"But I have this." Sam held out his phone. Ruan caught a glimpse of video, Clem's figure easily recognizable in the pale dawn light as he nailed up Linda's body to the sacred stone.

The silence, profound and charged, was broken by Wyn's shaky intake of breath. Slowly she reached over and took the phone from Sam's hand to start the recording again, watching it in a hush that made her second gasp a heavy thing like a morning star to the face.

"That's . . ." Sam had collected his own breathing. He sounded calm now, though a little otherworldly. Ruan had to wonder if he was dissociating through this whole experience. "That's the body of the latest girl who committed suicide. I *can* prove the cyberbullying, if you give me time to walk you through the evidence, but—"

"I don't need to see more than this."

Hunched over the screen, Wyn no longer looked queenly, her lips white and her face heavy, slumped like unbaked dough. "Boy," she said, locking eyes with Clem. "What were you thinking?"

Clem lunged for her. There was a ripping noise as the collar of his shirt tore, and Martin had to throw himself forward after him, grab him by his leather belt. Pulling him back, he got the other arm around his neck in a loose chokehold.

"I don't have to listen to you, you fucking old woman," Clem spat, struggling against the restraint. "I'm the new generation. People are already more afraid of me than they ever were of you."

Wyn passed Sam's phone to Harry, who watched it with Martin peering over his shoulder as Clem kicked his shins. Harry was shaking his head when he handed it back to Sam.

"You didn't listen to any of what I said before, did you?" Wyn asked. "About us being heroes, about us taking care of this town. People might fear me some, but they respect me too, and respect goes both ways." She jerked her head towards the far door, "Put him in the cell for now. And Harry? Phone Jennifer Gwynn and ask her to come down here and talk to me. I'm going to have to put this right."

Jennifer's phone was engaged. It took ten minutes on ringback before the cave's landline could get through to her, but half an hour later, Washcloth gave a bugle of joy as Jennifer's footstep sounded in the passageway door, and she stepped down into the room like she was familiar with it.

Her shotgun was over her arm, but the rounds were in her pocket, a combination of readiness and goodwill that Ruan appreciated. She stopped to stroke Washcloth's head and then, looking up at Ruan, froze solid. He remembered only slowly that he'd been headbutted and punched—that his face was swollen, bruised, and streaked with blood and oil.

"I'm sorry," Wyn said, before Jennifer could get command of her voice, and by the way Jennifer's head whipped round, it was clear an outright apology didn't happen often. "Putting the frighteners on you a little was just business, but I don't hold with desecrating corpses."

"I don't hold with letting people beat up my nephew," Jennifer gritted out. "Or slicing up my dog."

"How is Tiger?" Sam and Ruan asked together, smiling at each other after.

"I don't know. I been talking with the family. I haven't had time to check with the vet."

"All of that was Clem's doing," Wyn said, drawing off her gloves and setting them down on the table so she could rub the bridge of her nose like she had a sudden headache. "And I'm right sorry for it. What can I do to settle things between us?"

"Clem goes to prison," Ruan said. "For what he did to those girls. You should talk to them about how he hounded them. He's sick."

In the beat of silence that followed, he got the strong impression that he shouldn't have talked while his elders were busy. For the first time, he found himself with some sympathy for Sam's view that relatives could be a bugger.

"What he did to them," Wyn folded her arms and leaned back, unimpressed, "was no more'n saying some bad things and frightening them a bit. 'Specting him to go to jail for that is ridiculous. Maybe they shouldn't have been so sensitive." She narrowed her eyes at his indrawn breath, riding over the protest he wanted to make. "Besides, prison's out. My lads know I keep 'em out of jail, and that's non-negotiable." She turned back to Jennifer, dismissing him. "But what I can do is put him on one of our boats. No gadgets and no shore leave, just work. His foot won't touch land again until you tell me he's forgiven. And we forget the curses. They were nothing but a bit of fun between you and me. No harm done. Deal?"

"How can that be a deal?" Ruan insisted, keeping his voice whether they thought it was rude or not. "He gets a job with his family? How can that be justice?"

Wyn huffed a breath of a laugh. "You never worked on a cargo ship, did you? A hundred mile out at sea in a storm, with the bilges flushing back into the drinking water and all the food caught mould and your bunk wet from the condensation. Cold and dark and up three nights in a row with no sleep, waiting, hoping, praying not to be scuttled or blown onto rocks or capsized. Life aboard ship? It's just like prison but with a chance of drowning."

"What's more"—Jennifer's nod unsettled Ruan. Looked like she was mysteriously on Wyn's side in this—"if he goes aboard ship tonight and stays there for years with no internet, that's the end of the matter as far as the girls are concerned. Their problem is solved. But if he stays ashore, he'll probably get bail. He might get community service or the like. He didn't physically hurt anyone alive, and there are folks who don't believe bullying is any big deal. Even if they can follow the cyber part."

Ruan shivered. He couldn't deny that all of this made sense, but there was something about watching these two elderly women brushing aside the law, deciding on their families' fates like they might have been swapping recipes, that scared him. What else had they been quietly handling over the tea trays and the jam pans at the Women's Institute meetings that no one ever found out about?

"Clem is very young," Sam whispered to him, hiding his face from everyone else. "Maybe he has a chance to change?"

Sam had that angelic side to him, and Ruan couldn't blame him for it, but he felt this mercy was going too far. "That's nice for him, isn't it?" he hissed back. "But what about the girls? Fucking traumatized them, didn't he?"

Auntie Jennifer must have been having a similar train of thought. She scratched her silver hair and scowled at Wyn. "We'll agree to Clem going on the boats if you pay the vet's bills for my Tiger. And see Linda Tyhiddy's sisters put through college, and if there's any of these girls that he hurt who want therapy? You pay for that too."

Wyn scoffed. "I'll pay if there's any of them from the families," she said. "The others don't count."

"Yes, they *do*!" Ruan took a half step forward, making Harry clench his fists. Sam put an arm around Ruan's waist and rested his forehead on Ruan's shoulder, the edge of his smile like a banner of light.

Jennifer looked at the pair of them and laughed. "Outsiders count too."

"Oh, if you must," Wyn conceded with a scowl. "Deal."

CHAPTER TWENTY-NINE

"I don't know what to think of any of that," Sam said as they emerged out of a twisting stairway into a storeroom in the cellars of the Angel. "Did I have some kind of psychotic break and imagine the whole thing?"

"Seemed fairly self-explanatory to me." Jennifer had her phone in her hand and was already dialling as they closed the trapdoor behind them and edged out into the back corridors of the inn. A few steps along a corridor so narrow that Ruan's shoulders brushed both sides at once brought them down into the snug, where a smoky coal fire was smouldering and distant plates clattered amid an odour of fishcakes and old beer.

There was no one in the small room, so Ruan took the chance to wind both arms around Sam's waist and pull him close. God he was a long streak of sunshine. Just being pressed to him, two layers of clothes and all, made everything come right at once.

"No," Ruan agreed, trying to rest his face against Sam's hair but unable to find a spot where it didn't feel like the bruises would burst if he did. "I know what you mean. I thought I knew this town down to the last cobble, and this was going on under my feet all along."

"It's like being in a Mafia film." Sam shuddered again, dramatically, but when Ruan pulled away to look at him, he was smiling. "But at least it's over."

Then he seemed to hear what he'd said. His eyes widened and filled with fear. Here, away from the sky, their blue looked washed out, fragile. "I mean the bullying is over. And the curse that wasn't a curse at all. I hope *we're* not?"

It must have only been about an hour ago that Ruan had begged him to stay. If Ruan was more of a bastard, he'd have been hurt that Sam didn't remember that. But he probably did, didn't he? This was only the anxiety, needing to check it again in case something awful had happened in the meantime.

"We're only just starting." Ruan couldn't press hard, with his split lip, but he kissed Sam's lips anyway, hoping the gentle touch would get the message across. Sam's mouth opened to him, and his tongue stroked out to lap carefully at the cut, making it blaze up like a furnace over his whole face. Kind of painful, kind of tingly hot. He gasped and wondered where the nearest bed was. Home? The van?

Jennifer cleared her throat, and when that didn't work, she kicked him on the ankle with her stout walking boots. "That was Alana on the phone. She says the vet managed to get Tiger stabilized. He's going to be fine. Also the police've taken charge of Linda's body, so she's back under cover and decent now. Wyn will see the poor girl's buried again with full honours, you mark my words, or she'll have the Gwynns to answer to. I don't know how she's going to square the whole thing with the police, but that's her business."

Ruan and Sam separated just as one of the staff, hearing their voices, came in to ask what they would have. Jennifer sank down at a single table, and Washcloth, whimpering, curled up on the floor beside her feet.

"Meanwhile, this old lady's had too much excitement for one day." Jennifer leaned down to pet the dog, leaving it unclear whether she had been talking about Washcloth or herself. She smiled up at the waitress. "Will you bring the dog a bowl of water and me a pint of cider, please. And anything you've got that both of us could eat. Some kind of meat stew, and an extra plate for the dog?"

Seeing the steel go out of Jennifer took it out of Ruan too, and he wanted his home, his own bed, the comfort of his childhood around him. He couldn't give Sam's back to him—it would not have been a comfort if he could—but he could share his own. So when the barmaid looked to him for his order, he shrugged her off. "No, we'll see you later, Auntie Jen. Thanks for loaning Sam the dog, and for handling everything at the end there."

"What's family for?" She smiled. "And on that note, I'm going to phone around and make sure everybody's told who needs to be. You put it out of your head now. It's going to be a good Christmas after all."

"I can't believe it's nearly Christmas either." Sam's shoulders came down as they stepped out of the pub into the light of a pearly-grey noon. There was very little wind, and the silence was immense, almost as though they had not yet stepped from the world of legends into that of the mundane. Perhaps they'd taken a wrong turn under the earth and had come out in a dream equivalent of Porthkennack, some fairy replica of the real thing, painstakingly carved on the inside of a pearl.

"Am I really booked to do tarot readings at the winter fair?" Despite the calm, it was chilly enough to bring a pink flush to Sam's cheeks. His eyes sparkled at the thought of the fair, maybe amused again in memory of how Ruan had sold him to the *Gazette* like a great mystic.

"You are, certain sure." The dancing eyes and the smile brought out Ruan's grin, though he had to be careful with it because it stung. "We should go round the charity shops and find you an outfit. Something with stars or skulls. Pentacles, whatever you prefer."

They reached the bus stop that would take them down to the harbour without having to do the long trek through town, which Ruan didn't fancy right at the moment, with his face throbbing and the memory of imprisonment and terror in him. Better to wait awhile and then sit all the way home.

"It's not a magic show, Ruan," Sam insisted. "I don't think it would be dignified to dress up like a carnival wizard."

"No, that's fine." The wrangle in itself made him feel better. Just to sit in safety and bicker about nothing important was adding back the gloss of reality to life under the sun. "You find something dignified then, and I'll dress up. I don't mind being your exotic assistant. In fact, I've probably got ancestors who came out of the slave markets of glorious Istanbul. I'd be a natural for it."

The bus coming the opposite way passed on the other side of the street. Ruan watched it because he was kind of ashamed for getting even that close to *I'll be your lovely concubine*, and he couldn't look Sam in the eye.

Sam's laugh was a thing of beauty—easy enough for reassurance, but breathy enough to let Ruan know the thought had appealed. Ruan grinned at the distant bus hot-faced, where it had stopped to let someone out.

"I don't suppose I'll make much money?"

"I can't say." The person who had just got off the bus was muffled up for winter in a camouflage pattern scarf and a baseball cap. Ruan wasn't sure why the man had caught his eye, but he couldn't look away. "I been at one of those fairs before, and the fortune teller charged twenty quid a go. See five people and you'd have made . . ."

Whoever the man was, he was heading rapidly in their direction, face invisible under the shade of his brim, but the stride rang a bell. Where'd Ruan seen that dark, burly figure before? His breath had speeded, his body was urging him to get up, crowd back against the wall. Whatever he associated with this man couldn't be good.

"Ruan? What's wrong?"

The stranger was only ten feet away now, and when he raised his head, the light finally fell on his eyes. Ruan yelped and grabbed Sam's wrist. Shit! He'd forgotten this guy. The guy he'd seen walking away from his house the morning he found the dead crow on his door. Another fucking Lusmoore by the look of him. All Ruan's newfound peace, his sense of having got to the end and come out safe dropped out from under him along with the world.

"Can I . . ." Sam moved in front of Ruan, sandwiching him between himself and the wall. *Keeping me safe*, Ruan thought, absurdly touched, though this man approaching was twice Sam's bulk. "Can I ask you what you want with us?"

"I want to talk to your friend there."

Ruan slid sideways along the wall to where he could see Sam's expression. A luminous mix of fear and certainty, like a sparrow raising its tiny wings to defend her chick from an eagle. It twisted his heart with pride, and a determination not to let Sam take harm for his sake.

"I'm here. I'm listening," he said. Not volunteering anything. Not knowing what to say.

"What've you got to say about these shoddy tattoos, then?"

"Sorry?" Ruan slid fully out from behind Sam and took his hand, partly for his own comfort, partly because Sam was shivering. He ran the question through the context of the last few weeks and came up blank. "What? What has this got to do with you hanging dead crows on my door?"

The big man took his cap off and scrubbed the side of his thumb across his eyes, frowning. "I did see that thing on your door when I called round to talk to you last time, but I didn't want to get mixed up with all of that, so I went away again. I didn't put it there."

Ruan's second wind of alarm and confusion dissipated at the explanation. Occam's razor and all that told him that this simple explanation was actually quite plausible. And that was a relief, if only because this guy had some superb art visible on his neck and the back of his hands, and Ruan didn't want to think ill of someone with that kind of taste. "But then, why were you calling round at all. You're a Lusmoore aren't you?"

"Brix." The guy's grin was engaging enough that Ruan found himself shaking his offered hand without a second thought. "Brix Lusmoore. I own Blood Rush."

"Oh my God, I know that!" Ruan's fear had added a slight hysterical edge to the open-mouthed fanboying he was doing now. "I mean, I know the name and the art. I didn't know it belonged to you. I love your stuff! But . . ."

Now he had oriented himself, the beginning of the conversation abruptly made sense. "But I don't do shoddy tattoos. I'm proud of my work."

Brix snorted. "Oh yes? You want to explain why I've had two of your friends at my shop wanting repairs? Tattoos so new they'd barely healed, already so badly faded they might have been out in the sun for years."

Out in the sun? Ruan put his head in his hands and groaned. "I denatured the ink, didn't I? What a fucking idiot! I should have thought of that!"

"Is this because I asked you to put sunlight in it?" Sam asked, looking from Ruan to Brix like a man who is always hunting down more blame to take.

"Yeah it is," Ruan had to admit. "I should have remembered, but I was so fired up about magic tattoos that I forgot the ink wouldn't like it."

"'Magic tattoos'?" Brix repeated thoughtfully, and Ruan was torn between grinning, because he obviously liked the idea too, and scowling, because it was *his* idea, damn it. The owner of the best shop in the area shouldn't get handed *everything*.

"The girls were going through some dark times." Sam stepped into the pause, a little less shaky now Ruan had also calmed down. "We made a protective sigil for them with sunlight-infused ink, so they would have light close at hand wherever they went."

Brix flashed the charming smile again. *Maybe overdoing it*, Ruan thought. He didn't like that kind of attractiveness aimed at Sam. The guy was a stampede of charisma that would be hard to stand against. "I like it. You could put the sunlight in water, though. Use the water to dilute the ink and get the same effect, right? Without potentially warming your ink up and creating a health hazard."

"I suppose I could," Ruan agreed, pleased that Brix had fixed what he'd broken, but downcast at having made such an amateur mistake. What other things was he overlooking from inexperience and ignorance?

"Cheer up!" Brix clapped him on the shoulder, making him stagger a step. "Apart from the duff ink, I liked what I saw of your work. Nice design. Good clean lines. Got a portfolio?"

Ruan staggered internally now too as something inside him leapt with hope. He'd been resigned to learning his trade on his own by trial and error. Though *resigned* maybe wasn't the right word. He'd made himself want it because he'd thought it was the only thing within his grasp. But if he was handed the chance to learn from someone who knew the trade already? A bit of archaic nonsense about families was not going to get in his way. He'd dealt with the Lusmoores now and emerged in the right. He didn't need to be scared anymore.

"I…I…Yes, I have. At home. Should I get it?" All by themselves, his feet made a little rush towards home, though the bus was due any moment and he wasn't going to run. "I can get it now. Are you offering me a job?"

"Hold up." Brix made a tolerant gesture in the direction of Ruan's cut lip. "You look like you need to go home and get that seen to. Bring your portfolio round by the shop tomorrow, and if I like it, I just might."

"Oh my God," Ruan said again, ashamed of himself for letting it slip out a second time, but unable to stop it. "Thank you!"

"No worries." Brix crossed the road back to the opposite bus stop to resume the journey he must have interrupted when he saw Ruan sitting here, and Ruan and Sam's bus came a few seconds later. He rode home in a daze, only conscious of the edge of Sam's smile and his two hands enveloping Ruan's left hand in a cage of warmth as it lay on Sam's thigh.

The hall at home smelled of mulled wine spices when they took off their boots there. Strings of Christmas cards stirred in the draft, the glitter on them flashing in the overhead light.

"Oh, Ruan!" Ruan's mam said after she'd taken one look at his wrecked face. She ran forward to hold her hands on either side of his cheeks, afraid to touch. He saw the tears start in her eyes and couldn't have that.

"No, Mam, don't cry. It's been a good day, honest. I don't know how much Auntie Jennifer's told you?"

"Everything. I've just got off the phone."

"They did hit me, and they locked me up—"

"Oh, Ruan!"

"But Sam came and rescued me. He came right down under the earth, into the caves, and he kept me safe, Mam, when I was so scared. And he says he's going to stay with me. He's going to stay for good. So really I'm happy. I know that's not what it looks like, but—"

Oddly, they were all crying now. His mam and Sam and Ruan all together. His mam got in under his arm and hugged him round the middle, drawing Sam into the huddle with the other arm. They couldn't have stood there long—the kettle didn't have time to boil— but when they pulled apart again, the last lingering sense of unreality was gone from the world and things were solid again.

"Come on in and sit down," his mam said, dabbing at her eyes with her apron. "I'll lay another place for Sam."

Guiltily, Sam edged back towards the door. "I don't want to intrude. I'll just . . ."

And Mam got him by both wrists and pulled him in to where Da and Jimmy were exchanging bad jokes. Da gave Ruan a look of concern mixed with pride, and nodded in a way that meant *Good job*.

Mam sat Sam down and said, "You're part of the family now, son. I'm afraid you've got to put up with it. Tea?"

Sam pinked up over the nose, making Ruan want to go over and kiss the tears that were still brimming in his eyes. But Sam got himself together too soon for that, just met Ruan's gaze across the table with more adoration and wonder than Ruan could possibly hope to deserve.

"Tea." Sam parroted. Then he laughed, like something had loosened in him and he finally felt right at home. "Thank you. Thank you. That would be nice."

CHAPTER
THIRTY

Sam woke on Christmas Day to the scent of pine. He and Ruan'd brought a small conifer in from the copse, planting it in a seasonally painted plant pot they'd bought at the Hotel Metropole Christmas Fayre. Now it stood in the central isle of the van, just behind the seats, resplendent under two strings of tinsel and a "Victorian Yule" ornament they'd found lying in the sweepings of the hall after the "fayre" was over.

The shine of the tinsel—red with gold stars—teased Sam's eye as he opened it, smiling to find himself perfectly warm, drowsy as a cat in a sun-puddle, with Ruan's long arm wrapped around his waist, and Ruan's long body pressed against his back. The cheek resting in the dip between his shoulder blades was no longer burningly hot, the bruises having gone down to wine and green stains. Ruan's hair no longer woke him with its tickle along his spine, but sometimes he still dreamed of lying in a nest of black feathers, cherished as a raven's chick.

By the look of the sky through the windscreen, it was eight-ish, barely after dawn—but a strange urge to rise and throw off the bedclothes and tackle his life was on him; a feeling of renewed strength and purpose was clamouring for his attention, and he couldn't lie here and let it fade.

Carefully, he lifted Ruan's arm and slid out from under it, feet meeting carpet tiles and cold air. Since he'd earned a hundred and forty pounds at the fair, and Ruan's mam had promised him a tank full of chip fat in lieu of diesel, and since it was Christmas, he switched the heater on rather than shiver. While it warmed the place up, he took coffee and his laptop back to bed, found Ruan half-awake facedown in his spot, breathing the scent of his pillow.

That . . . the idea that anyone would like him that much? He didn't think he was ever going to get used to that. He hoped that in twenty years' time, Ruan would still be there to choke him up by somehow, mysteriously, thinking he was perfect.

When he managed to slide in to the edge of the bed, sitting, his back leaning up against the upholstered wall, Ruan yawned hugely and swarmed into his lap. Not, apparently with any intention other than falling back to sleep. Fond and amused, Sam put one hand in Ruan's hair and opened Skype with the other.

As always, his mother was immaculately dressed and poised—they got up at five regardless of holidays. The sight of her sent a prickling like pins and needles through Sam's whole body. He expected his throat to close, the usual ice pick to skewer his lungs, but when the first shock was over, it eased.

"Hello, Mum. I just wanted to wish you a happy Christmas."

Her look of surprise hardened into anger. "Are you contacting us to rub it in that you're not here? Because I would have appreciated notice that you were not coming. I've catered for you."

It did snag him. It did tempt him to feel guilty and sorry for being such a terrible, unthoughtful person, and anger for being made to feel guilty, and guilt about the anger. *I did tell you I wasn't coming. I told you that weeks ago. It's not my fault you didn't believe me.* But to get into that would be to get into an argument like a cage fight—that neither of them would win, but both would come away from bruised.

"I'm sorry," he said, not because it was true but because it got them off her script and back onto his. "I thought I would Skype so you weren't worried."

"Of course." She rolled her eyes as she reached beneath her escritoire for her cigarettes, "Because I wasn't at all worried after you cut me off last time. Honestly, Sam, you're so selfish, I don't know why I—"

Ruan's arm tightened around Sam's legs, and the brush of a kiss to his hip halted his automatic spiral at her words. He closed his eyes briefly and breathed in pine and coffee and Ruan.

"I found someone," he interrupted, surprising her into silence. He considered elaborating, but he didn't want to share Ruan, didn't want to hear what his mother might say, or to risk that she might say something so unforgivable he would never be able to call her again. "I made some money. I'm doing a lot better. I—"

"Are you coming home?" Perhaps she had sensed the finality of his tone, the strange new calmness, because her voice had turned icy, polished.

"No."

He loved her. That's why this hurt so much. That's why he recognized the hurt in her, as her face set rigid and controlled. But they had always unintentionally made each other's lives a misery, and maybe it was time to prioritize happiness for once.

"And that's what you phoned up to tell us, is it?"

I called to wish you happy Christmas because it's the season of good will, Sam began to seethe again. *I thought I said that first.*

"Are you going to tell us where you are?" His mother ashed her cigarette angrily in a solid silver ashtray. The thought of her storming down here, spoiling all this, made him come over cold.

"No."

Her lip curled in disgust. "Unbelievable." She cut the connection.

"Blimey." Ruan had put his nose and one eye out of the blanket and was watching the blank screen with a scrunched-up, confused look. "Happy Christmas to you too, missus." He rolled onto his back and yawned up at Sam, soft and rumpled and concerned. "You okay?"

He was, astonishingly. Already the aches across his shoulders, down his neck, and in his jaw were sliding away like chains falling off. No dissociation, no lost time, no panic. He was deeply proud of himself. To celebrate, he set the laptop on the floor and slid back under the covers with Ruan. "I might need a round of consolation sex."

"I think I can manage that," Ruan laughed.

About an hour later, Sam got up a second time to have a quick wash while Ruan rootled through the cupboards for something to eat. They were to have dinner and presents with Ruan's family, so he hadn't bothered to lay in supplies, and Ruan was whining about it, semiseriously.

"I told you, you have to eat more! The days of starving to death are over now. I got a job, you've got people coming up here for their fortunes. You can afford food, all right?"

The truth was Sam still tended to forget about eating, but even half-serious complaint was more than he wanted from Ruan on Christmas Day.

"All right," he agreed, stepping out into the clearing to rake up the ashes of the fire. "But I don't know what I can do about it now. The shops are shut."

Maybe he could . . . catch a fish that they could have for lunch? That was not going to happen—the fish in this stream were about the size of a fingernail.

Ruan giggled just as Sam heard the footsteps coming down from the main road. "Well, it's a good thing I told everyone you were an idiot, then." He waved to Tegan as she and Maryam ducked under the overhanging branches and wormed their way through the windbreaks, Tegan with a Tupperware box in her gloved hands, Maryam with a casserole dish.

"Ey up, Mr. Atkins." Tegan grinned as they sat by the fireplace with the nonchalance of people who feel at home. It struck Sam forcibly that that was what this clearing was—not just the van, but the campsite and the copse itself. It was home.

"What have you got there?" he asked.

"I got mince pies." Tegan held them out. "And Maryam's got pheasant and almond stew. The others should be up soon."

"Others?" Sam took a mince pie automatically as it was offered and then was brought to a halt by the burst of flavour in his mouth as he bit into it, buttery pastry and citrus-spicy fruit. Time to rig the kettle by the sound of it. He smiled up at Ruan with a headshake, not trying to cover up how much it meant that Ruan had arranged to have him surrounded by friends.

"Kasey, Sarah, Amanda." Maryam nudged the casserole into the side of the awakening fire. "We all wanted to say thank you. Our parents won't tell us exactly what happened, and they go all white when we ask, but it stopped. The messages—the troll? They went away. And we know it was you and Ruan that did it."

"We wanted to tell you that we know you helped us, and we're going to help you now." Tegan nodded. "So Kasey's da said can you come and fix his PC? He'll pay, right. And all our mams want tarot readings—except Maryam's, 'cause she doesn't hold with that. And Amanda's dad's cousin? He wants you to come and put a finding charm on his trawler, so he can find the fish before anyone else. But once all the other skippers know he's had that done, they're going to want it too."

Sam laughed, a little hysterically, not knowing how to handle this level of good fortune. And then it got worse. Jennifer and Alana strolled up the path where he'd cleared the fallen tree, Alana with a fruit cake and Jennifer with an earthenware cookpot of tomato soup, the other girls arriving soon after. Already it was starting to seem like a party, as Alana took charge of making sure everyone had tea, and Ruan put his arms around Sam like he could tell Sam was having difficulty keeping himself together.

"I talked to Brix," Ruan murmured into the back of his neck. "And he agreed that as long as he's okay with the technical stuff, we can design the charm tattoos together like we planned. You'd get a cut of that too. What I'm saying is, you can afford to stay."

"I want to stay," Sam choked. He'd already said that—he wanted to stay for Ruan. But now Ruan's whole family and town were making a claim on his affections, and he was terrified that if he let them in, he'd disappoint them all.

"Well, this little wood's my land." Jennifer smiled at him, then looked abruptly away, perhaps because she could see him shaking. "You coppice it for me, I'll consider that your rent."

"I'm . . ." Sam struggled with his breathing, his voice. How had this happened? He'd been alone. Even in the middle of the family of his birth he'd been alone all his life. "I'm just an outsider. I don't . . . Why are you—"

He didn't know what to say. He was going to burst into tears in front of everyone, and that would be . . . so embarrassing. No one would ever want to talk to him again. He'd wreck everything. He'd make them change their minds. And . . . he wanted this. He wanted it so much. He turned his face into Ruan's neck and hung on. He wanted to stop here with these kindly people. He wanted to belong.

Ruan laughed, cuffed him on the shoulder, very gently. "That's what I'm trying to tell you, isn't it?" he said, love in his voice like the risen sun. "You're not an outsider anymore. You're one of us. You're at home now, lover. You're at home with me."

Explore more of the *Porthkennack* universe:
riptidepublishing.com/titles/universe/porthkennack

a PORTHKENNACK CONTEMPORARY

Wake Up Call
JL Merrow

House of Cards
Garrett Leigh

Broke Deep
Charlie Cochrane

Junkyard Heart
Garrett Leigh

a PORTHKENNACK HISTORICAL

A Gathering Storm
Joanna Chambers

Count the Shells
Charlie Cochrane

Dear Reader,

Thank you for reading Alex Beecroft's *Foxglove Copse*!

We know your time is precious and you have many, many entertainment options, so it means a lot that you've chosen to spend your time reading. We really hope you enjoyed it.

We'd be honored if you'd consider posting a review—good or bad—on sites like **Amazon, Barnes & Noble, Kobo, Goodreads, Twitter, Facebook, Tumblr,** and your blog or website. We'd also be honored if you told your friends and family about this book. Word of mouth is a book's lifeblood!

For more information on upcoming releases, author interviews, blog tours, contests, giveaways, and more, please sign up for our weekly, spam-free newsletter and visit us around the web:

Newsletter: tinyurl.com/RiptideSignup
Twitter: twitter.com/RiptideBooks
Facebook: facebook.com/RiptidePublishing
Goodreads: tinyurl.com/RiptideOnGoodreads
Tumblr: riptidepublishing.tumblr.com

Thank you so much for Reading the Rainbow!

RiptidePublishing.com

ALSO BY ALEX BEECROFT

ABOUT THE AUTHOR

Alex Beecroft was born in Northern Ireland during the Troubles and grew up in the wild countryside of the English Peak District. She studied English and philosophy before accepting employment with the Crown Court, where she worked for a number of years. Now a full-time author, Alex lives with her husband and two children in a little village near Cambridge and tries to avoid being mistaken for a tourist.

Alex is only intermittently present in the real world. She has spent many years as an Anglo-Saxon and eighteenth-century reenactor. She has led a Saxon shield wall into battle, and toiled as a Georgian kitchen maid. For the past nine years she has been taken up with the serious business of morris dancing, which has been going on in the UK for at least five hundred years. But she still hasn't learned to operate a mobile phone.

In order of where you're most likely to find her to where she barely hangs out at all, you can get in contact on:

Twitter: @Alex_Beecroft
Her blog: alexbeecroft.com/blog
Her website: alexbeecroft.com
Tumblr: tumblr.com/blog/itsthebeecroft
Facebook: facebook.com/alex.beecroft.1
Facebook Page: facebook.com/AlexBeecroftAuthor

Or sign up to Alex's newsletter, and you'll receive *Under the Hill: Bomber's Moon, Buried With Him, The Wages of Sin,* and *Lioness of Cygnus Five* absolutely free: alexbeecroft.com/alexs-newsletter

Enjoy more stories like
Foxglove Copse
at RiptidePublishing.com!

The Secret of Hunter's Bog
ISBN: 978-1-62649-374-2

Back to You
ISBN: 978-1-62649-575-3

Earn Bonus Bucks!

Earn 1 Bonus Buck for each dollar you spend. Find out how at
RiptidePublishing.com/news/bonus-bucks.

Win Free Ebooks for a Year!

Pre-order coming soon titles directly through our site and you'll
receive one entry into a drawing for a chance to win free books for
a year! Get the details at RiptidePublishing.com/contests.

CPSIA information can be obtained
at www.ICGtesting.com
Printed in the USA
LVOW08s2125300817
546976LV00005B/745/P